I0587051

WICKEDLY COVERT

Wickedly Covert

J.F. LOWE

Seduction and Sin Publishing

Copyright

Wickedly Covert
J.F. Lowe
Published by Seduction and Sin Publishing
Copyright © 2022 J.F. Lowe
Edited by Bailey Macks
EBook ISBN: 978-0-6488818-9-6
Print ISBN: 978-0-6454991-0-0

All rights reserved. No part of this book may be reproduced, scanned, or distributed in any printed or electronic form without permission. Please do not participate in or encourage piracy of copyrighted materials in violation of the author's rights.

This is a work of fiction. Names, places, characters and incidents are the product of the author's imagination and are fictitious. Any resemblance to actual persons, living or dead, events or establishments is solely coincidental.

Warning: The contents of this book for a mature audience.

About this book

Funny how things had worked out, she went from hunting down him for killing her brother to him sitting beside her as the new recruit in the Bureau. Most would say it is their worst nightmare, but even a nightmare could not prepare them for this. A normal married couple, living a normal life in a normal suburb, working normal jobs...well, if you can call two undercover agents trying to bring down one of the world's largest human trafficking rings "normal."

Pose as a married couple, easy. Keeping things professional now that might be hard.

Chapter 1

It was a good day, Casey Anderson decided. The sun was shining, the bees were buzzing, and she was back on the job at the Special Crimes Unit. Vacations had always grated on her, and that was in the best of circumstances, when she was just chafing at the idea of the nation's most wanted committing heinous acts while she was lazing about. But to say that the circumstances of her most recent vacation had not been ideal would have been an understatement of biblical proportions.

She forced her hands to relax on the steering wheel as she finally pulled into a parking spot at the Bureau. It wouldn't do to let the past get into her head, not today. No, she was going to stride straight into the future and ignore all of that absolutely insufferable bullshit she'd gone through in the last year.

His name hung on her lips, but she wasn't going to give him the satisfaction of a curse. Just thinking about him made her blood boil, but at least she was blessed with a calling that let her channel that into something a little more productive. She'd go into the office with zest and verve, throwing herself into hunting down whatever sick bastard was on her plate this week.

But as she got out of her car and made her way down to the looming, nondescript building that housed the Special Crimes Unit, she saw a terribly familiar man leaning against the wall. Every ounce of him oozed casual nonchalance, but she saw the way that his eyes glinted when he finally noticed her. She knew just how tightly wound the man was, damn him, and just what it felt like when he finally let himself loose, double damn him.

"Ashton," she said, plastering a painfully fake smile on her face. To most people, it probably looked pretty convincing, but Ashton would know better.

Sure enough, he noticed, but then he just grinned at her obvious distress. The way his arms were lazily crossed, the way that he took in her utterly professional attire with a single undressing glance, it was beyond infuriating.

"Casey, fancy seeing you back here so soon," he said with a smirk, his wicked eyes boring into hers.

She held her tongue because responding was definitely the wrong move. She worked here, not him, but bringing that up was just going to sound petty and insecure, especially if things had gone well at Quantico for him.

And so she just decided to ignore the subject entirely. Besides, flinging barbs was easier.

"Have you figured out how to separate colors in the laundry yet?" she asked, her voice the very essence of sweetness.

Ashton winced. "Come on, it only happened once. Besides, I wasn't the one who broke the dishwasher."

Casey let out a slow, steady breath, struggling not to make it a hiss. It was remarkable, really, the way that utterly mundane domestic issues had a way of getting under her skin that all the wretched crimes of her job could not. It felt almost sacrilegious to care so much about the minor squabbles that stemmed from living together with a man for a few months, especially when standing in front of a place where hundreds upon hundreds of people were studying far more serious problems as she spoke.

And yet she couldn't shake it, and so she strode right on past Ashton, heading to the unassuming glass doors that led to her salvation.

But to her irritation, he fell into step beside her, slipping inside without another word. Perhaps it had been too much to hope that he was just here to piss her off. The idea that she would have to work with him...

Casey shivered, and not out of disgust. It was far too difficult to work around the man, and he damn well knew it.

"Morning, Charles," she said to the portly security guard that was sipping on his atrociously sugary coffee.

"Morning, Casey," he said absently as he scanned her card.

"And how are the kids doing?" Ashton asked as his badge was scanned. "Did Lina's recital go well?"

"Oh yes, it went wonderfully, Ashton," Charles replied with a big grin, his face lighting up. "Have a good day, you two."

And then they were through, heading deeper into the maze of offices and meeting rooms that made up the saner parts of the building.

"When did you get so chummy with Charles?" Casey grumbled, not tacking on the childish complaint that he was her security guard, as if she somehow owned him. It felt irritating to have someone else intruding on her life so completely, even if that person was Ashton. Especially if that person was Ashton.

"Oh, just while you were gone on your vacation," Ashton mused, quickly opening a door before Casey had a chance to do it for herself.

She gritted her teeth, as much to block out her yearning for his scent as to bite her tongue.

"So you've already had a few days of active duty under your belt while I was away. Good to see you haven't accidentally shot yourself yet," Casey said as she hurried ahead to ensure that she got to open the next door. Of course, she was then left holding it as Ashton sauntered after her, failing to speed up as she'd anticipated.

"I think you'll recall that my trigger discipline was quite good," he whispered with a wink as he passed her.

Casey didn't blush, but she most certainly did look around to make sure that nobody else had overheard that particularly lewd remark. Then again, it wasn't like anyone else would have any idea exactly what that meant or the hedonistic night it referred to.

Leaning in close, she hissed right back at him. "If I recall correctly, that's the night that you forgot to piss after and got yourself an infection."

Unfortunately, Casey had lost track of time and they'd already found themselves in front of her superior's office. At that exact moment, Carlisle stepped out with a bemused look on his face.

"Oh good, I thought I heard you two. If you're quite done, come on in." And with that, he turned around and disappeared into his office.

Casey and Ashton exchanged a look that was half irritation, half sheepishness and followed him in.

Carlisle's office was fairly drab by most accounts, adorned with all the blandest furnishings imaginable. There was a touch of personality here and there, mostly in the pictures that he kept on his desk of his children, but for the most part, it was exactly the sort of place that one might expect to find filing cabinets upon filing cabinets full of boring documents. That was technically true, but only if one conceded that most of the details of law enforcement were fairly boring in execution while being exciting only in the grand scheme of things.

Casey and Ashton took their seats in front of Carlisle, which profoundly disoriented her. It took a moment to place the sensation, but then she recalled meeting Carlisle in a diner right before going to hunt down Ashton. And seduce him. And maybe arrest him.

Funny how things had worked out, and now he was sitting here beside her, a new recruit to the Bureau in front of his new boss. Hell, maybe she'd get to watch him getting chewed out. That could be fun.

But then she also had to contend with the fact that Carlisle had called both of them in, and it surely wasn't for his own entertainment alone. With a sinking feeling, she realized that she might actually be asked to work with the bastard.

It wasn't intentional, but she found herself staring over at Ashton as he sat in the seat beside her. At a glance, he appeared completely at ease, but she knew him better than that. His long, languid posture concealed a paranoid tension and the ability to leap into action at a moment's notice, whether it be for violence or delights. For years, she'd fantasized about killing the man, and then when she'd finally hunted him down, things had taken a turn for the sexual. Of course, it helped that he definitely hadn't been the man who had killed her brother, as she'd erroneously believed for years.

"So have you two been adjusting well?" Carlisle asked, folding his hands atop his desk and peering at his underlings intently.

Ashton and Casey both made the same noncommittal sound at the same moment, which should have tipped him off, but damn the man, Carlisle could be willfully obstinate when it pleased him, and so he just continued to watch them politely.

"It's been... good," Casey lied through her teeth. No need to bring up that she'd just taken a vacation to get away from the insufferable bastard at her side. Great lover, but atrocious to live with.

"Quite good," Ashton confirmed, surely holding back some equally big caveats.

"Great," Carlisle said dryly as he glanced from one to the other, surely able to spot their sickly sweet sarcasm. "That's exactly the kind of energy that I need you to bring to this assignment." With that, he slapped down a pair of manilla envelopes before the two agents.

Casey could feel her heart sink. It was her worst nightmare, being forced to work alongside Ashton in a professional capacity. Well, at least she could take refuge in the fact that it would only be a job, and at the end of the day, she could go home and—

"Posing as husband and wife?" Ashton asked as he read his files, his eyebrows nearly meeting his hairline. Casey gasped, nearly tearing the binding of her folder as she opened it to make sure that he wasn't teasing her.

"To infiltrate a human smuggling ring known as Black Rose," Carlisle confirmed, reading the words that Casey scanned over and over, hoping in vain that they might morph into something else entirely. "A human smuggling ring which, you may note, is responsible for moving thousands across the border every year, selling them to God knows who. And they're ramping up in scale as we speak."

That was all it took for Casey to feel her priorities snap into place. Ashton fell into a distant second place of concern as she flipped through the files, reading about an organization that filled her with more loathing with every passing line. If there was something vile you could imagine, they had a finger in it. Black Rose chose the poor and powerless in other countries, enticing them with opportunities and promises that they had no intention of delivering. All they had to do was get on a boat and head to America. The old, the infirm, the young, the beautiful, they took them all, and they had a purpose for everyone. Organ harvesting, illegal adoptions to seedy individuals, and all the sex trafficking that one could ever stomach, all in one place.

"They're ramping up, you say?" Casey asked as she processed a spread of heart-wrenching photographs. And those were the lucky ones that managed to get away.

"Yes, we have reason to believe that they're planning on taking over some of their rivals within the next few weeks. The other organizations are reprehensible, but in relative terms, things are about to get a whole lot worse for a whole lot of victims if Black Rose takes the reins," Carlisle said grimly, his eyes locked on one of the pictures facing him on his desk. He was almost certainly imagining his grandchildren being among the victims.

Casey flipped back through the dossier, this time trying to figure out how her and Ashton were to be involved. But as always, Ashton did just the right thing to tick her off, and so he was one step ahead of her.

"It says here that we're supposed to act like a couple that wants to adopt a child," he mused. "I'm not sure we can make the most convincing of prospective parents."

Casey was about to give him some choice words when she saw the icy look in Carlisle's eye. "Somehow, I get the feeling that they won't much care how suitable your household seems," he said, his voice deathly quiet. "Do recall the nature of their organization, if it's not too much trouble."

Thoroughly chastened, the pair applied themselves to studying the files once more. Or at least, they did for a few moments before Carlisle slid something across the table.

"And here are your tickets. You leave today."

Casey and Ashton glanced at one another at the same time. The gravity of the situation was just beginning to set in for her. Not only was she going to have to spend time with this jerk again, but she was going to have to act like everything was fine, and there was nothing she could do about it.

"Fantastic," Ashton said in a monotone that echoed her sentiments completely, which just incensed her all the more.

"Wonderful," she added with the same utter lack of enthusiasm, just to make sure that he got the same message. Oh yes, this was going to be a grand old time.

Chapter 2

Ashton Malick was not feeling particularly optimistic about the future. On the one hand, he was being given a chance to make amends for his admittedly boorish behavior in the past, and he might even be able to save a lot of people in the process. On the other hand though, that was where the trouble was. Getting through Casey's prickly exterior was going to be a problem, and it was going to be a trial not to bring up all the shit that she had most definitely done wrong. And on top of that, there was the little detail about being entrusted with taking down an entire human smuggling ring with only a woman that hated his guts as backup. A very sexy woman who hated his guts, but still.

"What the hell is he thinking?" the woman in question grumbled at his side as they made their way out of the building at a steady clip. There was no time to waste if the times on those plane tickets were correct, and if Ashton was sure of anything, it was that Carlisle was always correct.

"Yeah, unbelievable," he said gruffly, mostly to cover up the traitorous note of giddy hope that threatened to break free. No matter how much the beautiful woman at his side irritated him, he was still hopelessly infatuated with her. Always had been, always would be.

"He wasn't being serious," Casey insisted as they stepped outside and straight into a brisk breeze. She shivered, and he had to fight back the urge to offer her his jacket.

Instead, Malick just sighed dramatically and shrugged. "He said we have to pose as husband and wife, and I'm definitely not gonna go against Carlisle's orders. Are you?"

She pouted. The damn woman pouted! Didn't she know what that did to his belly?

After a moment of acclimating to the chill, they hurried towards the parking garage. "Well, I definitely can't defy him, not while I'm on my probationary period," he said.

"What's the worst that could happen?" Casey asked with a snort. "Sending you back to Quantico for summer classes?"

"Prison, of course," Ashton said with a chuckle. It was still hard to believe that he'd turned from a wanted outlaw to an operative from the government effectively overnight, but there it was, and that was that. "Any violations of my terms, they send me straight back."

Casey huffed, looking pissed that he had to have an answer for everything. He could practically hear her berating him for it, and he wasn't ashamed to admit that it got the blood pumping. Casey was hot, but when she was mad, she was hot as hell.

Of course, the last thing he wanted was for her to know that he felt that way, so he covered it up as best he could, just like he had for all the time they'd spent together in the last few months.

"Oh well, looks like we'll have to live together for a bit now. Whatever will we do?" he said as they began to go up some stairs in the parking garage, taking two at a time.

And then she rolled her eyes. Dammit, he really shouldn't have looked at her at that exact moment. For whatever reason, every time he saw that his memories were drawn back to a very particular night where they'd made up after an argument the best way they knew how. He'd made some silly comment while they got down to business, and there she had been, her face next to his cock as she stroked him, rolling her eyes and sighing before making eye contact and sucking him off to the best orgasm that he'd ever experienced.

His cock was so hard that he thought it might rip right through his pants. This was going to be a problem.

"What the hell are you up to, Ashton?" she asked suspiciously. Leave it to Casey to read his mind like that.

"Dunno what you mean," he said under his breath, surreptitiously trying to adjust himself down there by taking three stairs at a time but accomplishing absolutely nothing.

"I mean, why the hell are you coming this way? I know that my car is the only one on this level."

"Ah, about that," Ashton said with a sheepish laugh as they came out of the stairs to an area of the parking garage where there was indeed only a single vehicle parked. "I figured that we might as well get started on all the domestic bliss stuff. You know, riding in the same car and all that."

Casey stopped, which forced him to stop as well and turn to face her. She stood with her arms crossed, looking exactly like the badass he'd fantasized about for the vast majority of his life. And more than fantasized about for a few blissful, hellish months. Best not to think about the havoc that the next few days or weeks might wreak on his libido.

"Ashton, do you not have a car? How did you get to the office?" Casey pressed, stepping closer and tormenting him with the faint scent of perfume. And then she poked a finger into his chest, which was just too damn cute.

"They wouldn't let me have a license. Flight risk, they said." Ashton shrugged, which belied just how irritated he'd been about the Bureau's decision.

For a moment, it looked like Casey almost sympathized, but then the mask of mild irritation covered her face once more. Shaking her head, she strode right past him and towards her car. After a moment, she called back over her shoulder, "Hurry up, we don't have time to waste."

Elated, Ashton hurried after her. One of the main benefits of being behind her rather than beside her was that he could remember an awful lot of things and not have to worry about her reading it on his face. For example, what he might have done to that behind in that very car. It was surprisingly spacious, and he didn't just mean the car.

When he reached the car and opened up the passenger's door, he was surprised at just how potent those memories were. Just the smell was enough to fill him with a longing for more than the animalistic fucking they'd enjoyed together, no matter how incredible it may have been. So much more than that existed between them, and when he stopped to consider it for even a single second, it all felt too much to bear.

Stooping down, he got in and noted that Casey was watching him with a smirk. Looks like she knew him better than he thought.

"Remembering old times?" she asked innocently, and it took more than a bit of self-control to stop himself from leaning over the console and taking her in a deep, possessive kiss.

"Good old times," he said nonchalantly.

For a moment, the barriers of irony and distance between them faded, leaving two people reflecting on a shared history alone. All the highs and lows, the twisted way they'd come together, and the pain of realizing they didn't fit together as easily as they'd hoped. It had been a bitter pill to swallow, and now they were forced to relive it all for the sake of thousands of innocents.

"It'll be easier this time when it's fake," Ashton pointed out, hoping to god that she understood him well enough to not ask for clarification. They really did not need to start this off with a fight.

"That may be true," she conceded, and then the moment was over, and she was turning the key. "I need to head back to my place to pack," she added tersely.

"Ah," he said, and nothing more. He still had enough pride to not ask if she still had his clothes or if she'd thrown them out in a fit of rage. On the other hand, those would come in especially handy right now.

After a moment of staring straight ahead, Casey turned to him and sighed. "And yes, I still have all your stuff. You'll be able to pack there as well, and I'm only telling you that because we're in a rush."

Ashton felt a cheeky grin welling up and didn't bother suppressing it. "Because if there was no rush, you'd keep it from me just out of spite and made me think that you'd tossed everything."

"Precisely," she said crisply, finally hitting the gas and peeling through the empty floor with an ear-piercing screech. "I'm glad we understand each other."

He couldn't help but chuckle. Oh, how they understood each other. Then again, that was half the problem. A little less understanding, and they might not wear on one another quite so much.

"The whites are still ruined," Casey said after what felt like a mostly peaceful silence of heading down the endless turns to the bottom of the parking garage. "You'll need to buy new underwear and socks."

It was really quite impressive how one could be both annoyed and nostalgic at the same time. "If I recall, that one was your fault." He couldn't help it, he simply had to point that out.

"Only because you failed to sort them as I asked you to," she said, utterly calm and in control, not even glancing over at him, not changing her tone at all.

Ashton could feel his blood beginning to boil. Again.

"You're awful," he grumbled as he looked out the window at the riveting landscape of concrete, concrete, and more concrete. Oh, look, a car. And now more concrete.

"And you loved it," she said, pitching her voice low and hitting him below the belt. She knew what that did to him, and she didn't care. Or rather, she cared and wanted him to be an impotent, horny mess that couldn't have her.

Ashton snorted as if he couldn't care less, which they both knew was a lie, but she was kind enough to let this one slide.

The remainder of the ride back to her flat was, by and large uneventful. No subtle jabs were exchanged, nor any that were a little less than subtle. In the silence, Ashton quickly found himself confronting the sobering reality of what they were about to do and the level of responsibility that rested on his shoulders. Maybe they'd just been trying to get under one another's skin to avoid thinking about that.

But it was what he deserved. These demands were nothing less than justified after the life he'd lived. Though it was true that he'd been hunted for the one crime he hadn't committed, he'd still been a right bastard in a hundred other ways, and if this could partially atone for that, then he was more than game.

Now the only problem was going to be making sure that his complicated feelings for Casey didn't get in the way of the mission.

Chapter 3

Casey didn't particularly enjoy airports, but waiting in line for security screenings damn sure beat rushing to pack in what might as well have been an unhappy marriage. Back at her flat, it had been like they were any ordinary husband and wife that loathed each other and were sprinting to pack on the day before a vacation that would ostensibly be packed with fun but would realistically just be so fast-paced that they never got a chance to actually enjoy themselves as they ran down the itinerary.

She took a deep breath, unsettled at just how detailed that comparison was. Things were really dire if she imagined that kind of thing with Ashton at her side. To distract herself, she ran through the next leg of their plan.

They were to be Adam and Eve Johnson. Ordinarily, that would have struck her as a profoundly poor pair of choices given just how fake they seemed, but that was half the point. They were to present themselves as being in obvious disguise, which did make sense when it came to people that would be buying children from criminals.

It was rather elegant when you got down to it. There was less pressure because everyone would know they were presenting an inauthentic front, they just wouldn't know what actually lay behind it.

As for their destination, it was some manner of chateau, an old estate situated squarely in the countryside. There would be no nearby assistance, which she understood, but still made her uneasy. The blueprints she'd been given by Carlisle were fairly detailed, but apparently, the new owners had made a few additions, so who knows how much had changed?

She glanced ahead at the line and saw that it wasn't moving at all. Typical.

Ashton looked supremely relaxed at her side, dressed like any other businessman on a work trip. He tapped his foot from time to time, the only sign that he was stressed. Somehow, his ability to maintain an almost entirely calm exterior both pissed her off and reassured her.

"So how did things really go at Quantico," she asked, at first just to distract herself and perhaps to get under her skin, but then she realized that she actually did care about the answer.

"Great," he said, too quickly for it to be the truth and lacking any of the dripping sarcasm that would have set her at ease. If he'd been dismissive, she would have just rolled her eyes and moved on, but the tension in him was uncharacteristic.

"Great, huh?" she asked, lowering her voice and pressing a little closer to his side, ensuring that nobody else could overhear. It was unlikely that anyone cared, but one could never be too careful.

Ashton glanced down at her, something inscrutable in his gaze. She could see pain as she searched his face, but that was nothing new. He was a man who was constantly in pain if one knew where to look.

"It was hard," he said, breaking eye contact and staring off into the distance. "Some of the instructors treated me differently. Not badly, just... differently. I think they all knew. Carlisle said they wouldn't be told, but I expect they found out the specifics anyway. After all, they are the FBI."

Casey nodded, considering his words. It wasn't every day that Quantico was asked to take on a former criminal and train him. It was entirely plausible that some of his instructors might have done a little digging and found out about his history with Casey and her brother. And some of them likely didn't believe that Ashton was actually innocent of that particular murder.

Neither of them said anything. They never did when it came to her brother, neither during their tenderest and most vulnerable moments nor during the most bitter of their arguments.

Casey cleared her throat. "Alright, how do you want to play this?"

Ashton casually glanced around, checking again to ensure that nobody was listening in. He then placed an arm around the woman who was to pose as his wife, a gesture of intimacy that the two hadn't shared in quite a while. And last time, if Casey's memory served, it had ended with some choice words and a few bruises of the wholly consensual variety.

"I figured we'd just do what comes naturally," he purred into her ear, raising the hairs on the back of her neck. Damn him.

"If I recall," she began with as bland of a tone as she could possibly manage, "what comes naturally to us is fighting like cats and dogs."

She could feel his grin even if she couldn't see it. "Exactly. We're very believable at it. Besides, it seems rather plausible that a couple of human trafficking dip-shits would be insufferable human beings that could barely stand to be in one another's presence."

It was so very vexing when Ashton was right.

Ultimately, the sluggish journey through the air-port was painfully uneventful. Mostly, Casey had just stressed about making sure that she responded cor-rectly when her fake name was spoken aloud.

Which was utterly ridiculous when you got down to it. She'd been undercover more times than she could count. Hell, there'd been years of her life when she'd lived a lie more than she'd actually been her real self, and yet this made her feel like she was a novice all over again.

Of course, she didn't actually want to examine the reason for that in any great detail, mostly because she already knew exactly what it was: posing as Ashton's wife. The way that his hand brushed against hers, the way that his shoulder pressed against hers in a calculated fashion and meant to appear completely unintentional, drove her mad.

It didn't mean that she actually wanted to marry the guy. Of course not! She didn't even want to spend the rest of her life with him in a more unofficial capacity. That would be ridiculous!

No, she was just feeling a little awkward because... because...

"Why on earth are you growling?" Ashton asked at her side as they settled into their first-class seats. "I know that you have high standards, darling, but I assure you that it doesn't get any better than first class. Look at all the leg room!"

Casey fixed him with an icy stare over the brims of her sunglasses, but he looked positively incorrigible.

He leaned in close, and she felt her cheeks ignite. His lips touched her ear, and then he paused for a moment, which really was the last straw.

"And try not to fall asleep. Remember that you snore, precious."

She had been mistaken. That was the last straw. As punishment, she vowed to not speak to him for the entire rest of the flight, which would be at least a good three hours if the weather was ideal.

True to her word, she said not a peep, but her irritation quickly faded from being the main reason. Contemplating the sins of Black Rose was enough to distract her, and then she was running down through the list of contingency plans that had been in the briefing. Naturally, none of those were foolproof, and they'd need to evaluate the situation once they arrived at the chateau. It was going to be a matter of quick thinking on their feet and identifying the best way to both catch the big shots and locate any on-site victims and any incoming shipments. Hundreds, if not thousands, of lives depended on every move they made, and as long as she didn't have to admit it aloud, she was willing to rely on Ashton's competence.

As they drew closer to their destination, Casey watched out the window and was only mildly surprised to see that it was in the middle of absolute nowhere. There was no way that they were going to land at a major airport, which did make sense from the perspective of Black Rose. Fewer people around meant fewer people that could sneak in.

Disembarking was a tense affair. For a moment, Casey worried that the entire plane might have been heading to the same destination as them and thus might have been in on the operation. After all, what other reason was there for so many people to be taking a flight out to the middle of nowhere?

But the reason quickly became apparent when the vast majority of the passengers hurried from the plane to board a bus that, from the branding, appeared to be heading to some sort of company retreat.

"Poor bastards," Casey and Ashton said simultaneously as they looked at their fellow passengers in this new light. They were all heading to a weekend of team-building exercises and motivational speeches. God help them.

But then they were alone, standing on a rural runway in the middle of nowhere, watching as the bus sputtered off into the distance.

"He did say there would be a ride waiting for us, right?" Ashton asked, looking around to make sure that nobody was near before he retrieved the pertinent documents from his suitcase. They weren't foolish enough to actually bring the folders from Carlisle's office, mostly because it would be exceptionally bad if Black Rose searched their luggage, but they had brought some abbreviated versions written in code. At a glance, they appeared to be nothing more than financial reports.

In the meantime, Casey looked around the tiny airport. The plane they'd come in on was nothing more than a typical passenger jet, yet it dwarfed the tiny cluster of structures that made up the terminal. A few workers were tending to the plane, but after the vast majority of the luggage had been hurriedly thrown onto the bus, the pace had dropped down to a crawl.

"Think any of them work for Black Rose?" she wondered aloud, watching one man in a safety vest that was sauntering over to the plane. Nobody was actually approaching the pair of visitors, but that meant little.

"Maybe not directly, but they're definitely paid to inform about any odd behavior," Ashton said absently.

"Or just threatened if they don't snitch."

Ashton glanced up at that. "No, I expect that they're paid somewhat handsomely by Black Rose. Motivating through fear is generally a poor idea in these kinds of situations. It may keep most people in line, but someone may get a brave idea and head to the police. Can't have that."

Casey took that in without a word, annoyed that she was already appreciating what Ashton brought to the table. She was coming at this like a fed, and his insight would be nothing short of invaluable. After all, she'd only played at being on the other side of the law, but he'd actually lived it.

"Hm. Yeah, it says that someone should be waiting here to give us a ride out to the chateau. Ordinarily, we'd have to be blindfolded for the ride, but we can avoid that with a bribe. Allegedly."

She listened to all that with half an ear. There wasn't a car in sight.

"Don't we look exceptionally out of place?" she asked, looking down at her expensive suit. She looked like a high-powered businesswoman, and it made for a comical image to see her standing in heels on a dirt runway.

"Yes, but it's probably part of their strategy," Ashton explained as he straightened out and hoisted the suitcases that held their shared luggage. "They want us to be on the back foot when it comes to the negotiations. That'll make it easier for us to trip up and incentivize us to make our purchases and leave quickly. If we're in a rush to leave, then we'll probably pay whatever they want."

Casey nodded. "And if my eyes don't deceive me, I do believe I see our ride coming."

Ashton followed her gaze, and she watched as a subtle transformation came over his face. She hadn't realized it before, but there had definitely been some true warmth and humor lurking around the corners of his eyes and in the quirk of his lips. Only when it was completely and utterly gone did she begin to miss it.

"Showtime," he said without any humor at all, and she knew that he had to be thinking about the lives that depended on their success here.

Chapter 4

Ashton watched with an eagle eye, stepping forward and putting himself slightly in front of Casey. Hopefully, she wouldn't notice and would just think he was being a competitive little shit and trying to toy with her.

God, the plane ride over had ruined him. With so much silence, he was forced to be alone with his thoughts, which was never a good thing. Now more than ever, he knew that he couldn't let anything happen to the fiery, determined woman at his side. If it came down to it, he was willing to do whatever it took to get her out of this alive, even if it meant sacrificing himself.

Fortunately, that was enough to elicit a snort from him. Who could have ever imagined that the Ashton Malick of old would one day have such strong feelings for a woman?

The vehicle finally reached them, a beat-up old pickup that instantly set his instincts on high alert. It certainly didn't look like the kind of car that would be permitted on the grounds of an organization like Black Rose.

Slowly, the truck rolled to a stop, the windows already down. An unshaven man in a trucker's hat leaned forward in the driver's seat and greeted them with a polite wave.

"You the Johnsons?" he asked, his accent a thick country drawl.

Casey and Ashton exchanged glances, confirming that they were equally suspicious of this turn of events.

"We are," Casey said, pitching her voice just a hair deeper, making Ashton blink. Damn, that woman found a new way to turn him on every day.

"Well, then get on it. I'm supposed to talk you up to the old Donning place," the driver said. "Your suitcases can go in the bed."

Ashton looked over to the bed in question, where there was a scattered assortment of tools for gardening and carpentry.

The Donning place? Interesting, that hadn't been in the files. Maybe that was what the locals called the place, but it was surprising that Carlisle hadn't included that detail. Or was this some sort of code phrase that only Casey was privy to?

Well, nothing ventured, nothing gained. With that firmly in mind, Ashton set their luggage snugly into a corner of the bed and opened the truck door for Casey, who hesitated for only a moment before getting in.

When Ashton followed her into the back seat, he got a pretty good idea of why she'd hesitate. It was not a particularly clean truck, to put it lightly. There were some fast food wrappers down near his feet, and he had to push what appeared to be dog toys off the seat in order to sit comfortably.

Once they were both situated and had their seat-belts on, Ashton recalled his comments from the plane about first class. Yeah, some extra leg space would do wonders right about now.

"The Donning place?" Casey asked as the truck hummed back to life.

In the mirror, Ashton watched the driver's face. Their eyes met for just a moment, and to his credit, the driver merely raised his eyebrow.

"That's right. The Donning place. Been abandoned since '92."

"Excellent," Casey said, easing back into her seat and obviously relaxing. "So, what information do you have for us?"

Ashton was about to ask her what the hell was going on when she got out her phone, quickly typed a message, and showed him the screen.

Code from Carlisle, it was only in my files, not yours.

In his mind, Ashton knew that it was a perfectly logical choice from the perspective of the Bureau, and it was even more logical for Casey not to have told him. Still, he couldn't deny that it stung a little.

She searched his face, her own unreadable, and then she began to type again. This time, it just said, Sorry.

Ashton sighed and waved it off.

Outside, they were descending down into a fairly thick stretch of forest. In the mirror, the driver watched the two of them with an amused expression.

When Casey noticed his look, she cleared her throat. "Carlisle said you might have some additional intel for us when we arrived."

The driver simply shook his head. "I'm afraid not. The company at the chateau likes to hire locals to drive out-of-towners down from the airport, but none of us know much more than that. A few years back, the folks there moved in and slowly renovated the place, but they only brought in outside contractors. It was a bit of a sticking point, with a bunch of us wanting for jobs, but what can you do?"

"Do you know what goes on at the chateau? What the company does?" Casey asked.

The driver was silent for just a beat too long. "No, but it obviously ain't anything good," he admitted. "Else, the feds wouldn't be all that interested, I reckon."

Should they tell him? It was always a tricky situation that. On the one hand, maybe he'd be horrified and eager to help them out if it meant stopping some truly reprehensible people. On the other, he might get terrified and run away, or in the worst-case scenario, he might even tip off the company, especially if he was afraid of them hurting his loved ones.

And that wasn't even getting into the possibilities of him being a double agent all along, working for Black Rose while claiming to help the Bureau, or the chances that he might get a hero complex and try to solve everything on his own, which would also bring their plans crashing down.

Ashton watched Casey go through those same mental calculations, and by the look on her face, she'd come to the same conclusion as him. It was simply safer for the man to remain ignorant.

The remainder of the ride was largely silent, with Ashton glancing back from time to time to ensure that their luggage was still safely in the bed of the truck. The road grew bumpier by the minute, and it would be just their luck for their clothes and hidden weapons to go flying after a particularly nasty jolt.

Lower and lower they went until the trees were towering over the road and blocking out the sun. Speckles of sunlight shone on the ground ahead, but it was mostly shadow. A fitting driveway to a den of iniquity and sin, all told.

It was difficult to maintain a sense of direction with how many twists and turns there were. The only thing that Ashton was sure of was that they were still steadily descending below the altitude they'd started at.

And then, before they knew it, they turned a corner, and all was blinding light. It took a moment for his eyes to adjust, during which he watched the driver and noted that he'd pulled down his sun visor. The man was used to the experience.

Outside, there was a rolling plain of perfectly manicured grasses, cut in sweeping stripes that wouldn't have looked out of place in front of a billionaire's mansion. In the distance, their destination loomed large.

The chateau must have been ancient, more than a hundred years old. Some places were built to be merely evocative of older styles, but there was a palpable aura to the place that called to times long past. He would have believed in an instant that it had been an old plantation if it wasn't for the small fact that they were still firmly in the northeast.

He memorized the layout, instantly doing calculations in his head. The fact that it was a massive clearing was surely not a fluke or whim. It would take someone a good half hour to flee from the house on foot, and they would be running over flat land that would allow anyone to see them from the upper story. There was a good chance that there was some pretty sophisticated surveillance equipment installed there and watching their approach at this very moment.

When there was still a good mile to the building proper, they approached what appeared to be a small collection of sheds, ostensibly the sort that would hold gardening equipment. The pair of men that were casually sitting outside were certainly dressed like they were nothing more than gardeners, but Ashton immediately spotted the bulge of firearms beneath their jackets. These were security guards.

As the truck rolled to a stop, the pair of men split up, one taking each side. It looked like nothing more than a casual stroll, and it may even have been interpreted as an admiring inspection if it weren't for the fact that the pickup really was an old beater.

"How's it going, James?" the man on the driver's side asked a bearded fellow that was clearly trying to look somewhat out of shape while being extremely fit. The padding in his jacket would have done a pretty good job of hiding his pistol as well if Ashton wasn't on the lookout for exactly that. Then again, maybe he'd wanted people to notice and be intimidated.

And then, for a reason that Ashton couldn't even begin to understand, he felt a pang of jealousy and settled a hand on Casey's knee. The man was attractive, and no matter how insane the thought was, he didn't want her to work her seductive charms on him.

But Ashton was no novice, and so he bent the moment of weakness to his advantage. He leaned into it, making it a possessive squeeze with a look of utter contempt for the disguised security guard.

"Not too bad, Kev," their driver said, following the interaction in the mirror.

Kev bent down to take in the scene in the backseat while the other goon went to check on the bed. It was clear that he'd been expecting these new arrivals, but it was equally clear that he was competent at his job, and nothing showed on his face but bland amusement.

"Taking a couple lovebirds up to see the old place, James? How much you two pay him?"

Ashton could feel Casey bristle at his side. She was likely incensed at just how flippantly they were being treated when they were supposed to be VIP's. And, granted, she was doing an excellent job of playing that part, but damn if this didn't make Ashton feel perversely at home. Ribbing from a couple of guys low on the totem pole, who were probably going to sit back down and wait around for nothing to happen for hours after this. It was almost enough to make him feel nostalgic for the old days. But only almost.

"Do your superiors know that you are speaking to us like this?" Casey asked icily, putting on a haughty tone that was a splendid touch. The chances of them ever recognizing her voice were low, but this would just make the odds even lower.

At that, Kev only looked over to his comrade, which finally brought Ashton's attention over to the man that was rifling through the bed of the truck. This one was much thinner, with a hawkish nose and a gaunt face that might belong to a junky. Presently, he searched through the garden tools, leaving the luggage in the corner completely untouched.

It was reasonable when Ashton thought about it. The men were likely under strict orders not to disturb the guests' belongings, which was likely to put the typical sort of person who might be in their position at a strange kind of ease. At least they aren't going through the bags, they'd be thinking, even as they grew annoyed at the delay.

An intimidation tactic, probably as much directed at the driver as themselves. Since the guy didn't actually work for Black Rose, then hell, they were probably checking to make sure he wasn't smuggling anything else in.

But soon enough, it was over, and the two men exchanged a quick nod. Without any further ado, James tapped on the gas and moved right on past the little checkpoint.

Ashton felt the doubts creeping in only once the moment was gone. They could have been caught there. Those two men could have spotted something amiss or recognized one of them, then they could have just pulled out their guns and ended them on the spot. All the planning, all his life up to that point, and it could have ended before he'd even had a chance to reach the weapons they'd stashed in their bags.

He let out a slow, rattling breath and glanced over at Casey, who looked as cold as ice. She eyed him, frowned, and looked back to the chateau that was rapidly growing closer ahead.

It was gonna be tough, Ashton realized. He was liable to get way too comfortable with these life-or-death situations, and if he didn't reel it back, who knows what kind of hot shit he'd get them into?

Chapter 5

By the time they pulled up at the end of the driveway and found themselves a hop, skip, and a jump away from the front door, Casey had examined every detail in sight and compared them to the blueprints that she'd already committed to memory.

It would seem that their intel had been mostly correct. A few buildings near the western edge of the estate hadn't been marked, but they looked prefabricated and thus could have been put up at any point. It certainly made for an ideal place to store a bunch of people that you were shipping in just for the occasion. She would have to tell Ashton about that later and figure out a reconnaissance strategy.

"Just a moment, I'll go tell the staff that you're here," James said, hurrying out of the car and heading straight to the front door. He ate the ground in long strides, and she wasn't quite sure how to feel about that. It would be an opportune time for him to betray them while their guns were still in the back, but then again, just about every time to betray them in the near future was going to be opportune. They were vulnerable here, and everyone knew.

She looked over to Ashton, who was looking at the chateau with a faraway look in his eyes.

"What is it?" she asked, as much to make conversation and fool any eavesdropping devices as anything else. In the meantime, her hand drifted down to the inside of her thigh, where there was a small pistol hiding, just in case.

"I was just thinking about all the places that I've worked at before. You know, in a less-than-legal capacity. I'm pretty sure none were this fancy," he said somewhat absently. Shaking himself back to the present, he caught sight of her motion and saw what she was doing. She worried that he would try to throw a fit about how he should have the gun, but then he just nodded approvingly. Hell, maybe this wouldn't devolve into spitting and yelling like cats and dogs.

"Ah," Casey said, feeling the reassuring grip of that tiny gun in her hand. In half a second, she could pull it and put two shots in someone within ten yards. Give her a full second, and make that four shots at fifty.

James knocked on the front door, which appeared to be immediately answered, though the door didn't open far enough to reveal who was inside. A few words were exchanged, then that was that, and James was headed back to the car, looking completely preoccupied with his own thoughts.

"Think they'll let us in?" Ashton muttered.

"They have to," Casey said, as haughtily as she could manage. "Nobody can pay as much as we can for their merchandise."

A little on the nose, but subtlety could be overrated.

When their driver reached the truck, he looked up at them with a look of more than mild perturbation. "They... they said you can come in." And then, he looked genuinely torn. "I'm not sure if I should tell you, but I heard noises in there. I think there were—"

"It's fine," Casey said quickly, hurrying out of the truck and moving to grab her luggage. She was a step too slow and on the wrong side, for Ashton beat her to the punch and had their things out in an instant.

No need to let the poor driver out himself as potential loose lips if Black Rose really was listening in. The urge to look up at the top floor and see if anyone was explicitly watching was tempting, but Casey managed to resist.

Without looking back at James, they made their way to the colossal front door, carved with an intricate rose. Their poor driver was surely debating the ethics of shouting out his warning about what sort of awful things he'd witnessed, so they didn't give his conscience a chance to get the better of him.

There were three quick raps on the imposing door, and then it cracked open. For just a fraction of a moment, Casey felt the weight of what she was about to do bear down on her, and then she was imperiously shoving the door open to force her way inside.

After all, it was what a conceited, self-absorbed slaver would do.

On the other side of the door, she expected to find a majordomo waiting for her, probably a gawky, scholarly sort. It was exactly the sort of man she imagined handling the front of the operation, probably a guy that wasn't too intimidating to look at.

And as she looked at the more than two hundred pounds of pure muscle that was looking down at her with anything but amusement on his face, she had no idea why she would have ever expected something like that.

They had a human wall manning the front door because of course, they did. And as he looked her over and dismissed her with a single snort, she fumed and watched as he looked over to Ashton.

To her surprise, Ashton held that level stare right back, and the majordomo almost seemed surprised at what he saw. The two men stared at each other, one lithe and familiar, the other a bulky brawler that could very well have been a boxer. They were of a height, which just enhanced the effect, and as Casey watched with bated breath, she wouldn't have even been surprised if they started swinging on the spot.

"Eve and Adam Johnson," she cut in before things could deteriorate too much. "You've been expecting us."

The majordomo glanced back at her, not quite with newfound respect, but with a measure of satisfaction, as if she was acting exactly how he'd expected. Which, when she thought about it, was the exact opposite of respect, but if she got her panties in a bunch every time someone disrespected her, then it was going to be a long, long mission.

"Yes, there is a room waiting for the two of you. I'm sure you want to rest after your long journey," he said flatly. It was not a question.

But, just for the sake of character, Casey frowned and tapped her foot. "I was under the impression that we'd be able to do our business and leave quickly. My schedule is quite inflexible." Which was a lie, and it would be devastating if he gave in to her whims and sent her on her merry way.

Instead, his lips just curled into the faintest semblance of a sneer. He got a good deal out of telling impertinent women no, she could already tell. It would be satisfying to force him to submit to her, but somehow, she got the feeling that Ashton might not approve of that. And besides, the man was revolting on a fundamental level.

"Very well," she huffed. "Let's see our rooms then and get this over with."

"Room," the man said flatly, then turned and guided them onward.

For the first time, Casey had a chance to glance around. The entryway was rich and ostentatious, which struck her as utterly expected. There were rich carpets and chandeliers, along with a row of extremely expensive yet gaudy art. There was no rhyme or reason to how the paintings were situated. All that mattered was that Black Rose could show that they had money. The idea of taste did not enter the equation when it came to demonstrating their worth as a seller of human lives, it would seem.

They were led down one of several hallways that led deeper into the house, each of which appeared to be much the same. Part of that was surely an elaborate technique for ensuring that the slaves wouldn't be able to easily navigate to the exits in the case of any escapes. Most of the victims wouldn't be kept in the chateau, but it was entirely likely that a few would be brought over to show prospective buyers, if nothing else.

"How gauche," Ashton whispered into her ear, less mocking the art than teasing his own lack of such knowledge.

Normally, she would have been torn between rolling her eyes and shooting him an icy stare. Given their current circumstances, she obviously opted for the icy stare. It can't appear like she actually had a friendly — if exasperated — relationship with her husband in a situation like this.

One, two, three turns later, and they were deep in the maze. They didn't go up the stairs, which did make for an interesting note, but then they were stopped in front of a door that looked like all the rest: mildly garish and rather sturdy. Good for stifling the screams of anyone inside, she reckoned.

"This will be your room for the duration of your stay," the majordomo recited, but then he looked at the pair of them with a look that bordered on a leer. "And since you two are husband and wife, you won't mind proving that. Loudly."

And with that, he turned around and walked away. It took a moment for Casey to even register that he'd handed the key to Ashton, then another moment still for the ringing in her ears to fade. There was no way he'd actually said that, right? There was no way that he'd actually told them to have sex to prove that they were married.

But he had, and Casey could feel a cold clarity coming over her. Very well, if they wanted to play games, then she would be sure to win.

"Come," she snapped as she took the key from Ashton and opened the door.

"Woof," he said under his breath as he followed her in.

Chapter 6

Ashton watched Casey prowl around the room like a caged animal. A furious caged animal, exploring the confines of her new prison before turning her attention to her prey.

It was a little embarrassing that the mental image got him so hot under the collar, and so Ashton busied himself with closing the door, ensuring that the major-domo had left, and setting their luggage in the corner.

The room was quite nice by his standards, but then again, his standards were certainly the lower between the two of them. Ratty motel rooms had been the norm for him, and sleeping with half a dozen snoring other men in little more than a barracks had Ashton watched Casey prowl around the room like a caged animal. A furious caged animal, exploring the confines of her new prison before turning her attention to her prey.

It was a little embarrassing that the mental image got him so hot under the collar, and so Ashton busied himself with closing the door, ensuring that the major-domo had left, and setting their luggage in the corner.

The room was quite nice by his standards, but then again, his standards were certainly the lower between the two of them. Ratty motel rooms had been the norm for him, and sleeping with half a dozen snoring other men in little more than a barracks had been only slightly less common.

But this room was richly adorned with a massive bed, several large armoires, entirely too many hand-carved nightstands for any room of people to ever need, and a series of paintings that ran the gamut from impressionist to realist. The lights could clearly be turned down to provide more romantic lighting, and that entailed a number of switches and buttons on a control panel.

Ashton narrowed his eyes. They weren't just trying to bury them with lavish wealth and make them feel like valued guests, they were also providing dozens upon dozens of places to hide every manner of listening device.

"This is going to be a pain," he muttered under his breath as he went back to his luggage.

"Sleeping with me isn't that bad," Casey snapped, her arms folded as she watched him with narrowed eyes. It was hard to tell if this was just part of the act or not, but it amused Ashton either way. Best not to show that.

Without a word, he unzipped his suitcase and directed her attention to a hidden compartment, from which he pulled out a jammer.

Casey blinked, the outrage draining out of her face. Interesting, it hadn't all been just a facade then. It was getting harder and harder to hold back that smile.

A few clicks and buttons pressed later, Ashton was quite sure that nobody could overhear them. Or see them, he thought with a shiver.

Turning, he sidled up right next to Casey, his hand running down her side. Ears might be listening if they talked at a normal volume, but there were ways to get around that.

"As long as we whisper, we should be fine," he purred into her ear. Her gooseflesh rose in response, and he didn't bother resisting the urge to stroke it. After all, they had said to prove that they were married, right?

"Are... are you really going to do what they said?" Casey asked, her hand reaching up to caress his cheek, holding him close. Together, they stared at nothing in particular, eyes unfocused as they fell into the moment.

"We must do whatever the mission calls for, no matter the cost," he whispered with mock seriousness, then as she started to twist around, he planted a tender kiss on her neck.

That froze Casey. She looked so perfect when dressed up, like she was ready to go to a boardroom meeting and hold some shareholders over the coals, but she would look even better out of it. Besides, the fantasy of having a powerful, independent woman servicing him had always been overwhelmingly attractive to Ashton.

"There hasn't been anyone since you." He knew the effect that would have on her and left it up to her imagination exactly why he was telling her. To her, it would probably come across as more of a pitiful sign of loyalty, but to him, it was nothing more than the reason for why he had an awful lot of lust built up and in need of an outlet.

"Oh?" Her hand snaked down and settled onto his cock, which had been painfully stiff more often than not since he'd run into her at the bureau. "Oh..."

The breathlessness in her voice made him strain even harder, something that he hadn't imagined possible until it happened. The reflexive sound at the back of his throat was entirely unintended, but based on how it made her shiver, he made a note to repeat it in the future.

"They want proof, so why don't we give it to them?" he asked, raising his voice just enough for it to be a growl. If someone were listening in at the door, they would hear.

"Are— are you sure?"

He could feel her resistance melting away. There was no possible way that Black Rose could imagine just how much they had done to help these two overcome their barriers. Both wanted to fuck, but neither wanted to admit it aloud nor to confront all the messy problems that came with going back to the way things were before, in the heady early days of their reunion.

But to do it as an act? To fuck each other senseless because it would save some human trafficking victims? A dream come true, nothing less.

Ashton couldn't hold back any longer. Whatever listening devices were still in the room and too sophisticated to be stopped by their jammer would just have to bear witness as the real jamming began.

He easily lifted her, hefting her weight up into something resembling a bridal carry but with far more groping. Her tiny squeal blinded him for a moment, the pounding of his blood in his ears too thunderous for him to hear anything else. The things this woman did to him should be illegal.

Before Ashton had a chance to recover, she took the lead, reaching up and pulling his head down into an awkward kiss. Casey couldn't even wait until they got to the bed, she needed to feel him against her, to see if her memories of their kissing were exaggerated or understatements.

It was both. It always was with them, and as they made hot, violent love with their lips and tongues, he reveled in the weight of her in his arms. He wanted to set her down on her bed and ravish her, but he also wanted to bask in how she was giving herself to him, submitting.

The former was much stronger, so he eased her down onto the bed with a little more force than was strictly necessary. Her moan of pleasure proved it the right move, and he could feel her fingers exploring the fabric of the bed below.

It was one of the most underrated aspects of making love in various places, or at least Casey believed, and she had thoroughly convinced him while they'd been together. The novelty of feeling a new surface against your back, beneath your knees, slipping through your fingers... would the sheets be soft or coarse? Thick blankets and airy comforters, firm pillows, or pillows so soft that you needed to stack several just to ensure you didn't sink down into them completely? It was what made every fucking unique and memorable.

Casey rolled and shuddered beneath him, and it took all of Ashton's willpower to pull away, but the allure of getting a look at her in this state was too much to bear. He could feel her mixture of soft femininity and hard muscle, could taste her fear and resolve, but he needed to see her hair fanned out around her. Even though he could smell her exertion and dedication, could hear her quiet desperation, he still needed that last piece of the puzzle.

Her dark eyes burned into his. They'd both had the same thought: stop the kiss and stare. Time stood still as he hovered over her, both quietly heaving and trying to hold their breath so that they could hear every little moment as if they might be able to hear the heartbeat of the other if they tried hard enough.

Her stare was dark, sucking him in, threatening to drown him. And, all things told, it wasn't nearly the worst way to die that he'd come across.

And while she stared, the romance above was counteracted by the raw physicality below. Her fingers were moving to his belt, and with sharp, deft movements, she unbuckled him. This was a woman that not only knew what she wanted but knew her way intimately around how to get a man out of his pants. Or, more specifically, she knew how to get this man out of his pants.

"Were there others?"

From the look in her eyes and the way her hand stilled, she understood. Had she slept with anyone else since him? It would hardly be unforgivable if she had, and yet...

"No," she breathed, and Ashton felt something inside him relax, a tension he hadn't even realized he'd been holding. In a twisted way, they had been faithful to one another, which filled him with butterflies like he was a foolish teenager in puppy love.

"Wipe that stupid smile off your face," she grumbled, but it was undercut by the fact that she was also fighting a tug at the corner of her lips.

Of course, all that vanished the moment that she finally touched his cock. Then, there was nothing but the pure sensation of the moment.

They fought and wrestled, eager to strip the clothes from one another and not caring how awkward it got in the process. Her fingernails tore three separate buttons from his shirt, and it was a damn good thing that he'd brought a few more extras than were necessary. Maybe he'd even poke and prod her about how he'd planned for this particular proclivity of hers later and been vindicated.

As if she read his mind and wanted to get her revenge, Casey's fingers closed around his length, tightening right up to the point of pleasure, then tightening a bit more. He groaned halfway through unclasping her bra. If he opened his eyes, he knew that he would see a look of mocking superiority, so he just leaned down for a kiss and sucked that beautiful pride right out of her.

With their hips moving of their own accord, it was only a matter of time before they found each other. Her nimble fingers guided him in, and he fit as if he'd never left. And in his fantasies, he truly never had. Every time that he'd ever stroked himself in the dead of night, it was her face that had haunted his thoughts. No distractions did the trick, all that he could use was a woman that couldn't stand to be in the same room as him.

And now he was finally going to fuck her once again. To say that it was a dream come true was an understatement of comical proportions.

"You know we're doing exactly what they want," he whispered, unable to resist getting a tiny rise out of her.

"You mean you're doing exactly what they want. This is all your fault," she groaned but still kept her voice low enough that nobody could hear. Then, to ensure that nobody thought they were up to any funny business besides the obvious, she moaned so loudly in his ear that Ashton had to pause.

"Fuck." It was shocking just how close she brought him to the edge of orgasm, but it simply wouldn't do to actually finish at this juncture, and not just because of the mission.

"Oh my, you were telling the truth about not having been with a woman since me. Poor, poor Ashton." The gentle mockery in her voice did not help things.

"Just... give me a second." He tried to steady his breathing but to no avail. The sheer pleasure that he felt at finally being reunited with her in the most glorious of ways was not abating.

"What's wrong, afraid that you'll—"

Ah, that did the trick. With the goal of shutting Casey up firmly in mind, he thrust and willed himself to last. And sure enough, her eyes unfocused, and her lips formed a tiny O.

And then neither of them could hold themselves back any longer. He found a rhythm inside her, but he didn't do it alone. Her hips bucked, and the entire bed frame shuddered as she rose to meet him. Her hands groped and clawed, and the way she plaintively pawed at his chest gave him the resolve he needed to see things through.

"We're... we're really fucking because they want us to. It's just for the mission," she gasped. It would have been like a splash of cold water if he wasn't damn sure that she was trying to convince herself more than him. Not that the proud Casey Anderson would ever admit that though.

"Or maybe you just want to prove that you can still tame me," he growled in that way he knew she both loved and despised, the former because of how it made her lose control.

Her legs wrapped around him, trapping his body. He had his tricks, but she had hers.

"Oh? You want me to cum inside you?"

Her eyes flashed open, and she fixed him with a stare that didn't even permit the possibility of disobedience. "You're going to cum inside me, and it's going to drip out onto the bed, so they know exactly what happened. They're going to send some poor servant in here to check, and they're going to find a mingling of fluids so thorough that they'll have no choice but to believe us."

Not the sexiest command she'd ever given him, but she was lucky that he was already past the point of no return.

"As... you wish," he said, dropping down to seal it with a kiss. She didn't even try to wrench herself away, and by some miracle, the gesture morphed into the tenderest of embraces. Her arms gently wrapped around his neck, and their bodies slowed to a crawl. Tightly controlled, languid strokes filled her and squeezed him.

When they finally came, it was as explosive as it was relieving. All that pressure that had been building up, all that tension between them, it all rushed out in the spasming of her core and the thick cream of his cock.

But that was only the beginning. The mission had just begun.

Only slightly less common.

But this room was richly adorned with a massive bed, several large armoires, entirely too many hand-carved nightstands for any room of people to ever need, and a series of paintings that ran the gamut from impressionist to realist.

Ashton narrowed his eyes. They weren't just trying to bury them with lavish wealth and make them feel like valued guests, they were also providing dozens upon dozens of places to hide every manner of listening device.

"This is going to be a pain," he muttered under his breath as he went back to his luggage.

"Sleeping with me isn't that bad," Casey snapped, her arms folded as she watched him with narrowed eyes. It was hard to tell if this was just part of the act or not, but it amused Ashton either way. Best not to show that.

Without a word, he unzipped his suitcase and directed her attention to a hidden compartment, from which he pulled out a jammer.

Casey blinked, the outrage draining out of her face. Interesting, it hadn't all been just a facade then. It was getting harder and harder to hold back that smile.

A few clicks and buttons pressed later, and Ashton was quite sure that nobody could overhear them. Or see them, he thought with a shiver.

Turning, he sidled up right next to Casey, his hand running down her side. Ears might be listening if they talked at a normal volume, but there were ways to get around that.

"As long as we whisper, we should be fine," he purred into her ear. Her gooseflesh rose in response, and he didn't bother resisting the urge to stroke it. After all, they had said to prove that they were married, right.

"Are... are you really going to do what they said?" Casey asked, her hand reaching up to caress his cheek, holding him close. Together, they stared at nothing in particular, eyes unfocused as they fell into the moment.

"We must do whatever the mission calls for, no matter the cost," he whispered with mock seriousness, then as she started to twist around, he planted a tender kiss on her neck.

That froze Casey. She looked so perfect when dressed up, like she was ready to go to a boardroom meeting and hold some shareholders over the coals, but she would look even better out of it.

"There hasn't been anyone since you." He knew the effect that would have on her and left it up to her imagination exactly why he was telling her. To her, it would probably come across as more of a pitiful sign of loyalty, but to him, it was nothing more than the reason for why he had an awful lot of lust built up and in need of an outlet.

"Oh?" Her hand snaked down and settled onto his cock, which had been painfully stiff more often than not since he'd run into her at the bureau. "Oh..."

The breathlessness in her voice made him strain even harder, something that he hadn't imagined possible until it happened.

"They want proof, so why don't we give it to them?" he said, raising his voice just enough for it to be a growl. If someone were listening in at the door, they would hear.

"Are— are you sure?"

He could feel her resistance melting away. There was no possible way the Black Rose could imagine just how much they had done to help these two overcome their barriers. Both wanted to fuck, but neither wanted to admit it aloud nor to confront all the messy problems that came with actually going back to the way things were.

But to do it as an act? To fuck each other senseless because it would save some human trafficking victims? A dream come true, nothing less.

Ashton couldn't hold back any longer. Whatever listening devices were still in the room and too sophisticated to be stopped by their jammer would have to listen as the real jamming began.

He easily lifted her, hefting her weight up into something resembling a bridal carry but with far more groping. Her tiny squeal blinded him for a moment, the pounding of his blood in his ears too thunderous for him to hear anything else. The things this woman did to him should be illegal.

Before Ashton had a chance to recover, she took the lead, reaching up and pulling his head down into an awkward kiss. Casey couldn't even wait until they got to the bed. She needed to feel him against her, to see if her memories of their kissing were exaggerated or understatements.

It was both. It always was with them. As they made hot, violent love with their lips and tongues, he reveled in her weight in his arms. He wanted to set her down on her bed and ravish her, but he also wanted to bask in how she gave her submission, putting her body under his power.

The former was much stronger, so he eased her down onto the bed with a little more force than was strictly necessary. Her moan of pleasure proved it the right move, and he could feel her fingers exploring the fabric of the bed below.

It was one of the most underrated aspects of sex in various places, or at least Casey believed, and she had thoroughly convinced him while they'd been together. The novelty of feeling a new surface against your back, beneath your knees, slipping through your fingers... would the sheets be soft or coarse? Thick blankets and airy comforters, firm pillows or pillows so soft that you needed to stack several just to make sure you didn't sink down into them completely, it was what made every fucking unique and memorable.

Casey rolled and shuddered beneath him, and it took all of Ashton's willpower to pull away, but the allure of getting a look at her in this state was too much to bear. He could feel her mixture of soft femininity and hard muscle, could taste her fear and resolve, but he needed to see her hair fanned out around her. Even though he could smell her exertion and dedication, could hear her quiet desperation, he still needed that last piece of the puzzle.

Her dark eyes burned into his. They'd both had the same thought: stop the kiss and stare. Time stood still as he hovered over her, both quietly heaving and trying to hold their breath so that they could hear every little moment as if they might be able to hear the heartbeat of the other if they tried hard enough.

Her eyes were dark, sucking him in, threatening to drown him. And, all things told, it wasn't nearly the worst way to die that he'd come across.

And while she stared, the romance above was counteracted by the raw physicality below. Her fingers were moving to his belt, and with sharp, deft movements, she unbuckled him. This was a woman that not only knew what she wanted but knew her way intimately around how to get a man out of his pants. Or, more specifically, she knew how to get him out of his pants.

"Were there others?"

She understood from the look in her eyes and how her hand stilled. Had she slept with anyone else since him? It would hardly be unforgivable if she had, and yet...

"No," she breathed, and Ashton felt something inside him relax, a tension he hadn't even realized he'd been holding. In a twisted way, they had been faithful to one another, and that filled him with butterflies like he was a foolish teenage girl.

"Wipe that stupid smile off your face," she grumbled, but it was undercut by the fact that she was also fighting a tug at the corner of her lips.

Of course, all that vanished the moment her fingers touched his cock. Then, there was nothing but the pure sensation of the moment.

They fought and wrestled, eager to strip the clothes from one another and not caring how awkward it got in the process. Her fingernails tore three separate buttons from his shirt, and it was a damn good thing that he'd brought a few more extras than were necessary. Maybe he'd even poke and prod her about how he'd planned for this particular proclivity of hers later.

As if she read his mind and wanted to get her revenge, Casey's fingers closed around his length, tightening right up to the point of pleasure, then tightening a bit more. He groaned. If he opened his eyes, he knew that he would see a look of mocking superiority, so he just leaned down for a kiss and sucked that beautiful pride right out of her.

With their hips moving of their own accord, it was only a matter of time before they found each other.

Her nimble fingers guided him in, and he fit as if he'd never left. His fantasies, he truly never had. Every time he'd ever stroked himself in the dead of night, her face haunted his thoughts. No distractions did the trick, all that he could use was a woman that couldn't stand to be in the same room as him.

And now he was finally going to fuck her once again. To say that it was a dream come true was an understatement of comical proportions.

"You know we're doing exactly what they want," he whispered, unable to resist getting a tiny rise out of her.

"You mean you're doing exactly what they want. This is all your fault," she groaned but still kept her voice low enough that nobody could hear. Then, to ensure that nobody thought they were up to any funny business besides the obvious, she moaned so loudly in his ear that Ashton had to pause.

"Fuck." It was shocking just how close she brought him to the edge of orgasm, but it simply wouldn't do to actually finish at this juncture, and not just because of the mission.

"Oh my, you were telling the truth about not having been with a woman since me. Poor, poor Ashton." The gentle mockery in her voice did not help things.

"Just... give me a second." He tried to steady his breathing but to no avail. The sheer pleasure that he felt at finally being reunited with her in the most glorious of ways was not abating.

"What's wrong, afraid that you'll—"

Ah, that did the trick. With the goal of shutting Casey up firmly in mind, he thrust and willed himself to last. And sure enough, her eyes unfocused, and her lips formed a tiny O.

And then neither of them could hold themselves back any longer. He found a rhythm inside her, but he didn't do it alone. Her hips bucked, and the entire bed frame shuddered as she rose to meet him. Her hands groped and clawed, and the way she plaintively pawed at his chest gave him the resolve he needed to see things through.

"We're... we're fucking because they want us to. It's just for the mission," she gasped. It would have been like a splash of cold water if he wasn't damn sure that she was trying to convince herself more than him. Not that the proud Casey Anderson would ever admit that though.

"Or maybe you just want to prove that you can still tame me," he growled in that way he knew she both loved and despised, the former because of how it made her lose control.

Her legs wrapped around him, trapping his body. He had his tricks, but she had hers.

"Oh? You want me to cum inside you?"

Her eyes flashed open, and she fixed him with a stare that didn't even permit the possibility of disobedience. "You're going to cum inside me, and it's going to drip out onto the bed, so they know exactly what happened. They're going to send some poor servant in here to check, and they're going to find a mingling of fluids so thorough that they'll have no choice but to believe us."

Not the sexiest command she'd ever given him, but she was lucky that he was already past the point of no return.

"As... you wish," he said, dropping down to seal it with a kiss. She didn't even try to wrench herself away, and by some miracle, the gesture morphed into the tenderest of embraces. Her arms gently wrapped around his neck, and their bodies slowed to a crawl. Slow, languid strokes filled her and squeezed him.

When they finally came, it was as explosive as it was relieving. All that pressure that had been building up, all that tension between them, it all rushed out in the spasming of her core and his thick seed from his cock.

But that was only the beginning. The mission had just begun.

Chapter 7

"You're sleeping on that side," Casey said with a gesture to the deep, evident stain where she'd been lying moments before. It would have been nice to bask in their carnal reunion for a little while longer, but then she would have to confront feelings and questions that she'd rather not.

Ashton blinked, then just shrugged and took it in stride.

"You don't even want to spend five minutes enjoying the afterglow? Isn't that a thing that women like?"

Casey ignored him completely. The issue at hand was whether to put back on the clothes that they'd just ripped off one another. It would certainly send a message, showing up outside with circumstantial proof that they'd carried out their appointed task. Would it be too much though? Would it seem like they were trying too hard?

"New clothes," Ashton said decisively, reading her mind and heading over to the luggage in the corner.

Casey considered that, but it made for a good excuse to head over to the various armoires and give them a look inside, ostensibly to decide where to store their belongings. Still, more to check if there were any unpleasant surveillance devices in the area.

Or something even more dangerous, but they could cross that bridge when they got to it.

"Maybe you should mess up your hair a bit more. They'd believe you then."

She gave him a look over her shoulder, but Ashton just grinned lazily at her. He still hadn't put his shirt back on, and the bastard knew what that did to her. Against her will, her eyes drew down to the sleek musculature of his chest. The man certainly hadn't slacked on working out since she'd seen him last. If anything, he was even more built.

"My, my, someone's trying a little too hard," she said dismissively, then turned back to her task. Unfortunately, it was trivially easy to find and remove the little listening bugs hiding in the corners of the shelves and drawers so she couldn't distract herself from the man behind her.

And that was before he had the audacity to saunter up behind her, place a hand on the small of her back, and gently slide it down until it was caressing her cheek. And then, he went a little lower.

"Still dripping, are we?" he whispered.

It was infuriating how much he could turn her on even when she didn't want it. And yet she couldn't resist leaning back against him. He wouldn't get a single peep out of her, not a luxurious sigh or a sweet nothing. It was bad enough that she rested against him like he was some sort of pillar of stability, enjoying his warmth and his scent, but there was no way that she was going to give in any further than that.

And the sex didn't count. That was just for the mission.

The moment eventually ended when she realized a way to turn the tables. So he wanted her to look like she'd just rolled out of the fucking of her life, did he? Well, two could play that game.

Turning her head, she kissed his shoulder, then his collarbone. Slowly, she worked her way inward, peppering him with fluttering pecks of her lips.

And then, when she got to his neck, she planted a deep, sucking, erotic kiss. To distract him, her hand ventured downward, exploring just how ready he was for round two.

Ashton was hard as a rock. Perfect.

Pulling away, Casey admired her handiwork, both in the naked need on his face and the growing hickey on his neck. Perhaps he could cover some of it with his shirt collar, but that would just enhance the appeal. After all, a bit of redness peeking out was far more provocative than a blatant mark of their work.

It took a moment for him to realize exactly what she'd done, but he knew better than to trust her when she got that smug smirk. Just like that, he snorted and went to get dressed.

Strangely enough, Casey felt the urge to follow him, to apologize, and she hadn't even done anything that needed apologizing for! But he'd looked so much like he wanted to be with her that it couldn't help but tug at her heartstrings.

Instead, she just turned around, went to her respective luggage, and suddenly realized that they might not be able to leave at all tonight. Easing just a little closer to Ashton, low enough that only Ashton could hear, "Can you check if there's a guard out there? Are we prisoners for the evening, expected to attend a meeting, or free to roam?"

To her surprise, Ashton simply nodded and moved to the door. She'd expected a bit of backtalk, or at least a mocking joke or two, but he did precisely as she'd asked. It was almost enough to make a special agent's heart flutter.

He rapped on the door quickly, then pushed it open. There was little chance that anyone could see Casey unless they stepped inside, but she still moved a little further out of sight, putting a heavy dresser between her and the door.

"Fancy that," she muttered as she plucked off yet another bug that this new angle had allowed her to see. There was little chance of it transmitting information because of the jammer, and it would reinforce the fact that they were experienced guests to the Black Rose, but more than anything, it was just satisfying to crunch those little shits.

Little bits of metal and plastic fell to the floor like dust as she rubbed the tips of her fingers together.

After what felt like an eternity but was surely no more than a few moments, the sound of a voice could be heard on the other side.

"Yes, sir? How can we be of service to you?"

Not the majordomo from before, but this one sounded deeper and a little less sophisticated. Perhaps a piece of hired muscle by the sounds of it.

"I was—" Ashton began, then caught himself before he could sound something as silly as polite. That wasn't how a couple slaving assholes would talk to the help. Clearing his throat, he began again. "When we will be meeting the sellers and seeing the product. My partner and I are only here for a limited amount of time and are very busy."

It was less of quiet chuckling on the other side and more of blatant guffawing. "Oh, I'm sorry sir, I didn't want to interrupt you as you already sounded busy. Not to worry sir we are discreet about our guest's sexual provocativities. I must admit though, sir, we had a bet going on whether you'd go through with it because of, let's just say, her provocation or whether you would chicken out. She seems rather a handful."

Interesting. Casey had no idea if this was him being rude to a guest because he was an incompetent, crass sort of if it was some masterful gambit by the Black Rose to intimidate them and put them on the back foot. She was leaning towards the latter because if it were the former, then their job would likely get a lot easier and a lot messier, and she couldn't rely on that.

Still, if the organization was this lacking in discipline, then maybe they could find a servant or two that might get them the information they needed.

"You didn't answer my question," Ashton said with the perfect blend of impatience and dismissiveness. "Are all the staff here so rude and incompetent?"

Casey held her breath, unsure if he would take it as an insult and if he was bold enough actually to do something about it. With a sinking heart, she realized that there were probably an awful lot of people here that he had been treating like absolute shit without any repercussions. If nothing else, it was a strong indicator that some of the human trafficking victims were indeed nearby.

"Of course, sir, there will be a small gathering tonight. Formal, of course, a few buyers are joining us before the main event. Our boss will be unable to attend though. Please come on out whenever you're ready, and someone will show you the way. But do feel free to continue with your lovely woman should wish."

Ashton coldly shut the door, blocking out the rumbling laughter that followed. However, when he turned to Casey, he was contemplative.

It was becoming second nature to step closer to him, to intrude on his personal space, every time she wanted to speak and be heard by him alone.

"What are you thinking?" she murmured.

"I'm thinking that they're watching us pretty closely if all we have to do is step outside to indicate that we're ready for whatever meeting they've got arranged for us. Our odds of sneaking out and reconnoitering the place are pretty low, for now at least."

Casey nodded at that. "Then we are agreed? We should go to this dinner and get a feeling for the others?"

"Yeah, we might even be able to play some of them against the others. With any luck, we can sow some seeds of chaos for later. That might provide some cover when we actually execute our plan, whatever it may be."

Reasonable, which was a tad annoying to Casey. She'd wanted him to say something mostly correct so that she could offer a slightly superior recommendation, but those were her thoughts exactly. The man was deep inside her head, among other places.

"Now, what would a couple of assholes looking to buy a human or two to wear to a dinner party?" he mused.

It was a rhetorical question. Both immediately retrieved the formal wear they'd brought specifically for this occasion. She had an emerald dress with a plunging neckline, ideal for capturing the attention of anyone that they wanted to manipulate. He had elected not to go for a tuxedo, reasoning that it would be a little too much, and based on what they'd seen so far, Casey wasn't sure if that had been the right call. The place around them was gaudy, and it might do to blend in and appear like they had just as little taste as the slavers themselves.

Still, they managed to get dressed in record time. Makeup was applied, and mirrors were shared, but soon enough, Casey and Ashton were facing one another and searching for anything out of place. Or, in Casey's case, looking to see if that hickey was still visible.

It was, to her everlasting delight. No amount of starch would make his collar tall and stiff enough to cover the telltale mark that she'd left.

His frown told half the story, and the devilish look in his eyes told the rest. "I shouldn't be the only one looking like I just had the time of my life," he said, looking her up and down with more than a little unguarded appreciation. By the path of his eyes, she could see him tracing her every curve.

It was odd how strong the urge was to tug her dress both down and up, wanting to cover her legs and chest a little more. The way he looked at her made her feel uncomfortable on a fundamental level, and she was damn sure that it would be easier to have the heartless monsters out there leering at her breasts than Ashton.

"We never really did this," she said, realizing how silly it sounded only after the words left her mouth.

Ashton grinned at that.

"The whole 'getting dressed together before going out to fancy dinners together,' I mean, you idiot."

His grin just grew wider at that. "I knew what you meant. I just think you're adorable when you're awkward and frustrated."

She stared at him flatly. "If I'm frustrated, it's because you didn't do a good enough job earlier."

His wink was infuriating but also cut straight to her core and made her feel an echo of the tingling from before. Both knew that he had done an excellent job of tending to her needs.

"We were always too busy staying in, fucking, and eating takeout instead," he mused, absently stroking hair away from her face. "No big date nights out for us. Besides, they probably would have frowned on you consorting with the likes of me in public."

Casey reached up to readjust her bun, but he stilled her hand and did it for her. The way his fingers felt against her scalp was heavenly. Too heavenly.

It was a strange state of affairs when it was far easier to turn about and storm out into an estate full of human traffickers than to confront Ashton, but there you had it, and that's precisely what Casey did.

A fraction of a second before she twisted the doorknob, Casey schooled her face to snooty arrogance. If they were watching the door as keenly as she feared, then she couldn't let her guard down for even a single second.

As she stepped out into the corridor, she quickly did a count of the doors. There were only a dozen or so rooms in this hallway, but it was impossible to tell how many there were in the entire building. The old architectural plans in the briefing had said there were a hundred, give or take, but if renovations had been made, that number could fluctuate wildly. There was a good chance some walls had been knocked down or rooms partitioned to isolate the victims even further.

As expected, a young woman promptly appeared at the end of the hallway, dressed so much like a French maid that it looked more like a Halloween costume than actual professional attire. As she drew closer with a pained smile plastered on her face, Casey realized that she looked more than just young. She couldn't have been more than fifteen or sixteen, and by how carefully she was stepping, she wasn't used to the extremely impractical shoes.

Casey exchanged a glance with Ashton, whose expression had instantly shifted from mildly amused to dark and stormy. Good, he understood the message that was being sent to them: this was what they could buy if they won the bidding.

"H—hello," the girl said with a nervous curtsy, not quite managing to make eye contact. "If— if you don't need anything else, then I can guide you to dinner."

The way the girl subtly emphasized anything else eradicated any misgivings that Casey might have had. The offering was clear, and she was being forced to do it. They were definitely in the right place, and the intel had been on the money about Black Rose.

"Show us the way," Casey said sharply, offering her arm for Ashton to take. It was good to get into the rhythm of him being her chivalrous escort going forward.

The young maid glanced between them, barely able to contain her relief. It broke Casey's heart, but there was no way that she could offer comfort, not when they were being watched at this very moment. She had to remind herself that she was going to be helping many more girls like this by sticking to her guns and showing not an ounce of compassion in public.

Casey raised an eyebrow, which startled the girl. "Right, sorry, this way!" she said quickly, her skirts fluttering as she spun about and hurried down the hall that she'd just come from.

Ashton watched her without a lick of lust. If her heart was heavy, she could only imagine how much worse it was for him. After all, the implication had mostly been that he would be the one who might desire a roll in the hay with a young thing that was still squarely in puberty.

Without any further ado, they followed the maid at a respectable pace as befitted a pair that thought themselves superior to everyone else. Of course, it was just a pleasant side effect that they got plenty of time to memorize precisely how many intersections they went through (three), exactly how many doors were down each of the hallways that split off (far too many to search without a concrete direction to start with), and how many other people were out and about inside the estate (half a dozen maids, nobody else).

It was too much of a risk to whisper her thoughts to Ashton, so Casey simply hoped that he would be thinking along the same lines as she was. It would be risky, but if they could manage to corner one of those servants, then they could probably secure some real answers. The issue was going to be finding one that was scared enough to ask for help but not so frightened that they might get flighty and decide that their chances were better off by informing on them to their masters. A tricky situation indeed.

Ultimately, they were led to what had to be the west end of the estate, where an open door led to a small congregation. They could hear the voices inside, low and good-spirited, before they could see anyone. As they drew closer, it was clear that it wasn't genuine mirth but the practiced laughter of people that didn't trust or even like each other but had to put up appearances.

"Enjoy your evening," the maid said, curtsying and trying to scurry away before Ashton caught her by the arm.

"What's your name?" he asked, sounding as bored as possible.

The poor girl's eyes widened with fright, and when she spoke, it came out as little more than a squeak. "V—Veronica, sir. If you want me to come—"

Ashton opened his mouth, then closed it and frowned.

"Yes, do come by later," Casey cut in. "You look like you might be fun."

Ashton shot her a glance that would have been unreadable to anyone but her. It looked like irritation, but she saw the gratitude lurking under there. It was difficult to intimidate this poor girl, but it was also the only lead they had, and if she had to suffer under the misapprehension that she was going to be abused, then that was a price that they were willing to pay. As long as she didn't get abused, that was.

Her eyes still wide, the girl barely managed a jerky nod before turning and fleeing. If Casey wasn't mistaken, she'd been fighting tears by the end there.

Oh yes, Black Rose had a great deal to pay for.

It was tempting to stand in the doorway and try to get a peek at what might be going on inside, but that was the behavior of an FBI agent or a woman that wasn't confident in such a setting. No, to make this look real, she had to act like the whole world should be kneeling at her feet.

Casey swept into the room, Ashton hurrying in her wake. Interestingly enough, it appeared to be a sort of larger apartment rather than a formal eating space. There was a living room, which they were now entering, and it was attached to a small kitchen and eating area, where the other guests seemed to be gathered.

That was why she hadn't been able to see all of them from outside.

It was a peculiar arrangement, but it did make sense in a building of this size. It also suggested that the inhabitants here were more of the long-term variety, so this might give them some leads on actual members of the organization or some regular buyers.

Chapter 8

They had just an instant before the table full of rich assholes noticed them, but it was enough for Ashton to get a good read on exactly who he was dealing with.

And they were definitely rich assholes. Oh sure, there was some variety in the exact type of rich asshole, but it was an umbrella that they were all tightly clustered under.

Three women were sitting and drinking wine while two men stood in a corner, speaking intensely but in hushed tones. The ring on one of the women — an older lady with distinguished gray hair and an extremely conservative blue gown — matched the ring on one of the standing men. A couple then, or at least they wanted to appear as such.

The other two women were a study in opposites. One thin as the other was broad, the former redheaded and laughing with emerald eyes, the latter a sober woman with a square jaw and an imposing physique. Both looked up at the newcomers with sudden interest, but his attention was already moving to the two men, who ordinarily would have posed the most immediate threat.

However, one glance was all it took to confirm that he wasn't in much danger on that front. While anyone could pull out a gun or knife and end you on the spot, these two fellows were anything but imposing. One was an older gentleman, about the same age as the woman wearing the same ring as him. In other circumstances, Ashton would have readily said they were husband and wife, but the fact that he was posing as a married man was not lost on him.

The second man looked downright sickly, coughing into a handkerchief that he held with trembling hands. He looked about two inches away from needing to wheel an oxygen tank around. Either it had been a much more rousing conversation than Ashton had initially thought, or he needed to take it a bit easier.

All that assessing took a matter of moments, and Ashton and Casey were smiling politely, expecting to be introduced like the selfish dipshits they were playing.

"And who do we have here?" the redhead asked, perking up and looking at the pair with barely concealed glee. Predatory glee, if Ashton's instincts weren't mistaken. The way she was eyefucking could not have been less subtle, and it made him feel as dirty as Casey's attention had made him feel valued. Resented, but still valued.

"Adam and Eve," Casey purred, her voice just that hair lower. Once more, he felt a chill run down his spine. He would really need to ask her to use that voice in the bedroom if they ever had to prove their loyalty through intercourse again.

"Ah, the new bidders," the older woman said, her voice surprisingly smooth and resonant. He wouldn't have been surprised one bit if she was into singing.

"And I suppose that makes you the old bidders?" With a hint of entitled irritation, Casey said that Ashton decided it wasn't entirely manufactured. She was probably getting a little annoyed that there was a woman already eyeing him like a prize while her options in the male department were quite a bit more limited.

Then again, Ashton wasn't sure if she was barking up the right tree. While still silent and maintaining a stern air, the third woman at the table did appear to be evaluating Casey quite thoroughly. Now that he got a good look at her, he decided that she wasn't quite as unattractive as she'd first appeared. A little outside his usual tastes, but it wouldn't be too terrible a fate to watch her and Casey enjoy themselves in the name of the mission.

"That it does," the man that didn't look like he was about to keel over at any moment said. "But please, come and take a seat!"

What ensued was a decidedly surreal experience for Ashton. A few names were exchanged, but he expected that they were about as real as his own cover. As far as he was concerned, Red, Square, Gray, Emphysema, and John were perfectly workable names. What could he say, the other guy just looked like a John to him.

For the next handful of minutes, they complained about the food and service, musing about the country-side and their trips over to the estate. It was the most mundane of details, and while he was fairly certain that none were outright lies, they were all carefully chosen and crafted to reveal absolutely nothing about the speaker.

By the end of introductions and small talk, he was finding himself almost at home among them. It was easy to imagine that they were random strangers chatting at a bar, but then he brought himself back to the moment and realized that these were five people here to buy what amounted to human slaves. In the best-case scenario, they would just be used as unpaid labor. And he didn't even want to think about the worst-case scenario.

Casey had fallen into conversation with the women at the table, leaving him to join the two men as the conversation returned to its state prior to their arrival. As such, he discovered precisely what the two men had been debating so vigorously before he'd appeared.

"You would think they would... pardon me," Emphysema said before turning away and coughing hoarsely. "My apologies, as I was saying, you think they would have more medical staff on hand, given everything they're doing here."

"Quite right," John said with a nod. "One would think they would have plenty of doctors on hand to deal with all those nefarious diseases they might bring over."

Ashton nodded politely, but it was damn hard to keep a straight face. The sheer callousness was astounding, and he got the feeling that this was about to get a lot worse before it got better.

For a moment, Emphysema raised a finger, and Ashton wondered if he was going to be pleasantly surprised. Was he actually going to say that they shouldn't be quite so inhumane?

"And the diseases are just the tip of the iceberg! The worst part is how they breed like rats! Rats, I say!"

"Rats," Ashton repeated, then muttered a "charming" under his breath as he drank the wine they'd so thoughtfully provided him. He hadn't thought that anyone would see, but John's lip was quirked in something resembling a wry grin. He too, took a drink.

Soon enough, Emphysema was ranting and raving about the gravest ills in the world and how they all came back to poor foreigners, and he certainly didn't mean that they had a hard lot in life.

It was rather impressive, the way that he could go on and on, working himself into a frothing rage while having to stop every few words to cough and excuse himself. The most astonishing part was that nobody even disagreed with him. It was merely murmured agreement and increased drinking from Ashton and John, but Emphysema just plowed ahead.

Ashton glanced back to the women's table to see if anyone was following this. Not a single pair of eyes were turned in his direction. In three of those cases, he expected that they were simply used to this man's diatribes. As for Casey, he was thoroughly impressed at her ability not only to ignore the shocking words but also to feign the perfect mix of boredom and interest in the idle chatter of the other three women.

Of course, he knew far better than to think that the women were as harmless as they appeared. It was calculated, the way that they were mentioning things they'd done and people they knew. Subtle clues meant to mislead one another, perhaps giving insight into who they were and bragging about their connections, perhaps just trying to force someone else to reveal a juicy bit of gossip. It was positively exhausting.

"Excuse me, I really must go find my personal physician. Tomorrow, gentleman," Emphysema said, making his departure after a particularly brutal coughing fit.

And then there was just John and Ashton, watching him make his way out of the room. As wrong as he knew it was, Ashton felt a bond with the man beside him, forged in the strange fires of listening to a wild and unhinged rant. Then again, he did have to remember that this man started it with his comment about diseases. Still, it was all a matter of relativity sometimes.

"Would you like to go out on the balcony and smoke? The view is actually quite lovely out here," John said suddenly, gesturing to one of the doors leading deeper into the apartment. Ashton had assumed that it had just led to the bedrooms or a bathroom, but this was an interesting opportunity to do a little more reconnaissance.

"Lead the way," he said, glancing back to ensure that Casey saw where he was headed. Her finger tapped on her glass in acknowledgment, so subtle that he would have missed it if he hadn't been paying careful attention. Then again, the other three women were probably watching just as closely. He'd just have to trust that she could handle herself there. It wasn't like he had any other choice.

Soon enough, he was out on a balcony with John, though it was both an exaggeration and an understatement to call it that. They were still on the ground floor, so it was more of a porch than anything else, but the odd landscape on this side of the house changed everything. There was a rolling slope below, so even though they were on the ground floor, one could still fall quite a ways if they decided to take a tumble off the side. Or roll, rather. It would be less falling and more like a long, bumpy road to the bottom.

John had pulled out a pack of smokes, and the box looked surprisingly cheap, which was to say that it looked normal, but the juxtaposition with all the surrounding opulence made them seem inferior.

"Your favorite brand?" Ashton asked with a nod. He didn't recognize the packaging.

"Indeed, can't get them on this side of the Atlantic," John said, pulling one out and lighting it. "Want one?"

"Nah, I quit a while ago," Ashton murmured, still focused on that last statement. He didn't detect an accent, so maybe it was just a case of Americans liking foreign brands to appear more sophisticated, but...

Ah well, nothing ventured, nothing gained.

"I take it you're not American," he said.

"Guilty as charged." John sighed in satisfaction. "What gave me away? I thought that I'd managed to smooth out my accent."

John snorted. "Just a lucky guess."

For a time, they stood in silence. It was impressive how little they could hear from inside the kitchen even though the pair of doors were still open. Then again, that seemed more like a feature than a bug if people got up to have as much fishy business as Ashton expected in these rooms.

"You're not really here to buy any merchandise, are you?" John asked casually.

Ashton felt his blood run cold. There's no way that they'd been found out already, right. It had to be nothing more than a probing strike, a shot in the dark as retaliation for his own guess.

"It depends entirely on the level of quality," he replied, meeting the level stare of a man whom he may have to kill in a few moments if it came down to it.

Though Ashton had stashed away a small knife in his sleeve for the occasion, the rolling slope beside them did make for a useful way to get rid of an inconvenient body, especially if he could make it seem like the bastard had gotten drunk and fallen off in a stupor.

John moved a little closer, and Ashton found himself evaluating exactly how strong the man might be. Even if this fellow got a lucky shot in, he was confident that he could still disarm him and choke the man out in a matter of seconds. Breaking necks was overrated, but smashing windpipes was always on the table.

"I only ask because I think we might be here for the same reason," John murmured. The man was stone-cold sober. There was no way that the story of him being drunk would be bought.

"What do you mean?" Ashton asked, his throat dry.

"I mean that we're here on behalf of a foreign intelligence agency in order to dismantle the Black Rose operation and end their human trafficking. And I'm guessing that you're here for a domestic agency, probably the FBI."

Never before had Ashton been gripped by such a mix of shock and relief. He had been found out, but it may turn out to be the stroke of luck that they needed. If allies were to be had here, they could pool their resources and take down these slavers. But whether or not they were allies was still a big if.

"You and that woman in there? Is she your partner?" Ashton asked.

"Ah, you noticed. The ring gave it away?" John wondered, taking a long drag and smiling. "You're a sharp one. I think we'll get along famously." At that, Ashton could hear the faint hints of a British accent.

"The ring gave it away," he confirmed. "I take it you're not married."

"Oh no, we are. Different rules for fraternizing agents over there, you know how it goes."

"Really? How fascinating," Ashton said, suddenly wondering if they were being monitored. Even if this man was who he said he was, this could still end in disaster if they were being surveilled. And hell, maybe it was just an elaborate trap to make him admit his own aims to someone who worked deep in the Black Rose.

Some of that must have shown on his face, for John glanced around. "Give me a second, and I'll show you proof. And don't worry, this is my apartment. It's been cleared of bugs."

Chapter 9

Casey found herself deep in her element. The other three women — Erika, Olya, and Artemis — had proven excellent sources of both intel and confidence. The longer she chatted and sparred with them, the more it reassured Casey was in her own disguise.

When Ashton had wandered off with Artemis's husband, Casey had already been deep in discussion with Erika about the merits of various types of servants. The redhead was quite sure that girls who didn't speak a word of English were ideal because that meant that not only could they not overhear anything they shouldn't, but that they also couldn't run away and seek help from anyone else that didn't know their tongue. As such, she enjoyed picking up servants from Asia and Africa.

Reprehensible stuff, but it fit in entirely with what else Casey had learned about the woman so far. She was a young heiress who simply had no concept of what it was like to actually lack money or be anything but society's elite.

Olya was a bit more interesting. The woman was obviously considering whether or not she wanted to flirt with Casey, and she was quite sure that if the woman did set her mind to it, then she would be extremely forceful and blunt about her desires. It could be an interesting source of further information but not one that Casey wanted to pursue quite yet, so she feigned ignorance for the most part.

As for her interest in their whole reason for being with Black Rose, Olya seemed to be a middlewoman for some shady industries in Eastern Europe that were always looking for more labor sources. Casey got the distinct impression that anyone purchased by this woman would be used rather brutally, and she wasn't sure if that was better or worse than the sort of sex trafficking that she'd envisioned. After all, a nasty mining gig in Siberia wouldn't be a pleasant experience for anyone.

But that did open up some very interesting questions. Prior to meeting Olya, Casey had been pretty sure that the trafficking operation was mainly dealing in the sort that was easy to cow and keep captive. There was much more to consider if they were also trading in strapping young men.

And then there was Artemis. It was extremely difficult to pin why she was here, and if someone in the group was a mole for the Black Rose — and she was damn sure that somebody was — then Artemis was a perfect choice.

She was relatively quiet and watched everything with interest. Though her hair was gray, Casey suspected that she wasn't quite as old as she seemed. Maybe she dyed her hair, or perhaps she had gone gray prematurely, but Casey imagined that she couldn't have been older than in her forties.

As for the topics of conversation, they had drifted around which types of wine they preferred, how taxing the journey had been, and how attractive Ashton was. Or, to be more specific, Erika had gone on and on about how she wanted to get him alone, obviously looking to get a rise out of Casey. Which she had of course provided, albeit in a muted and sulky fashion. Hopefully, it wasn't too obvious that she was just playing along, but Erika seemed satisfied with her manipulations and results.

"But I am afraid that I must be going," Olya said after a prolonged silence, taking her glass and downing it. Her eyes narrowed, she watched Casey for a moment, contemplating her choices, and then rose to her feet. "Until we meet again."

Before she had even completely left through the front door, Erika sighed loudly. "It's a shame what sort of people they allow in here."

It was nothing near a slam when the door closed, but it was forceful enough to make one wonder. By Erika's smile and the way that Artemis shook her head, this was rather the norm.

"You needn't antagonize her so," Artemis said, taking another sip of her wine.

Erika narrowed her eyes, obviously calculating if she should pout and act annoyed at that. "But it's so entertaining. And just wait until she figures out that I spiked her drink."

Casey kept a straight face, marveling at her good fortune. Her very first night here, and she'd already found two buyers that were at odds with one another? A little manipulation, and she could likely turn their little spat into a full-blown distraction.

"No, you didn't," Artemis said.

"Of course I did. Nothing serious, mind you, just something to give her some trouble on the toilet tonight," Erika said, barely holding back from cackling with glee. It was honestly a difficult contest to judge when it came to insufferably: this redhead versus that old nutcase from earlier.

"No, you didn't," Artemis repeated more forcefully this time. "I watched you all night, and you didn't do a thing."

Erika opened her mouth to reply but came up with nothing. Wisely, she shut up and looked away with a sulk.

And it was true, at least since Casey had shown up. She'd been vigilant for any sort of tampering with the drinks, not only for herself but for anyone else. Honestly, learning if one of the three was poisoning another was much more useful intelligence than finding out that someone wanted to drug her.

A knock sounded at the door, startling all three of them, but none showed it.

"Yes?" Artemis said. Near the beginning of the evening, Casey had gleaned that this section of the apartments belonged to her and her husband.

The door opened a crack, and a voice sounded from the other side. "Miss Erika? Your evening activities are ready."

Squealing like a little girl, Erika leapt to her feet and clapped her hands. She was a whirlwind as she gathered up her scattered belongings, stuffed them into her bag, and rushed from the room. Not even so much as a goodbye, but Casey wasn't exactly surprised by that.

And then there was just her and Artemis, the most dangerous of the women. For a moment, they both simply pondered the door, thinking about what sort of activities Erika might have had planned. Some sort of full spa experience, serviced by a variety of fit young men and probably torturing some poor servants. Imagining Veronica's face made it that much easier for Casey to hate Erika, but it's not like that was very difficult.

"An interesting pair, don't you agree?" Artemis asked. Now that they were alone, the woman's posture had shifted slightly. She was leaning a bit more forward, just a hair less reserved. And now, she was taking larger sips of her wine, which had stayed remarkably level throughout the evening.

"I agree," Casey said, holding her glass of wine that had gone equally undrunk.

Artemis looked contemplative for a moment, then looked in Ashton's direction, and her husband had gone. Gerald, he'd introduced himself as, but she was confident that it was just as fictional as Adam, Eve, and Artemis were.

As if on cue, the pair of men wandered back in. Both looked extremely serious, and Casey had to wonder if she would need to fight for her life in the next few seconds. If Ashton could take out the man, she was sure that she could reach her pocket pistol and defend herself.

"We can trust him," Gerald announced, taking the seat vacated by Erika and directing Ashton to sit where Olya had been.

"And her," Artemis added, giving Casey a meaningful look.

"Trust us with what?" Casey asked, but from the look Ashton was giving her, he already knew. He already knew, and he didn't quite know what to think of it.

"Casey," he said, which set off every alarm bell in her head. Why the hell was he using her real name? "They're British agents here for the same reason we are."

"Well, shit," Casey muttered under her breath. "Guess the cat's out of the bag then. They already know our names?"

"If it makes you feel any better," Gerald said, "I'm John, and this is Miranda."

For a reason that completely eluded Casey, Ashton choked on the water he'd just started drinking.

"And you're here to take down the Black Rose?" Casey asked, still not entirely sure if she needed to kill someone right now. Hell, offing Ashton for making such a stupid decision was feeling pretty justified at the moment.

"We are, and we're going to need all the help we can get," Miranda said. "This thing goes a lot deeper than you expected.

"Shit," Casey repeated, and then she started to drink the wine.

Chapter 10

Over the course of the next several minutes, Ashton found himself gripped by relief and hopelessness in equal measure. The latter because of just how insurmountable their task now seemed, and the former because he realized just how many traps they might have fallen into if they didn't pay careful attention.

John and Miranda had been infiltrating Black Rose for years and had already assembled detailed blueprints and schedules for the upcoming days. It was clear that none of their original plans to snoop around blindly would amount to anything more than being caught by the numerous patrols that lurked in the hallways. While there were definitely a number of cameras and microphones hooked up throughout the old building, the real threat were the armed Black Rose members that stalked through the halls at night. Even if one managed to elude them, they would still be hunted down by the state-of-the-art thermal sensors installed by the organization.

But therein laid a new kernel of hope. While thermal sensors would thwart practically any infiltration efforts they might make, if Ashton and Casey could manage to subvert and co-opt those systems, they would have an easy route for finding where most of the victims were being held. That was one of the few things that John and Miranda had been unable to discover.

"But there is an opportunity coming up," John said, interrupting Ashton's vague wondering about how they might break into the security control center. "There will be a large event held tomorrow, a surprise to many of the newer and smaller buyers that have been invited out here. However, the older and more established partners of Black Rose were given some warning as a courtesy."

"How many buyers are there total?" Casey cut in.

It was Miranda who answered. "Likely in the low hundreds, but that doesn't necessarily mean that there will be that many here. Some will have sent represen- tatives instead."

Ashton nodded. "So what's the opportunity then?" He met Casey's gaze and saw that she was clearly a little worried about him trusting these alleged allies so easily. Well, that made two of them, but it wasn't like they had any better options right now.

"On the surface, it will look like nothing more than a masquerade ball, an elaborate party thrown by the fab- ulously rich to mingle and demonstrate their wealth," John said, leaning forward intently. "But that's just on the surface. In one of the rooms, an auction will be held. A few partygoers will trickle in and out over the course of the evening, but it won't be random. Those will be all the biggest and most influential buyers and their representatives, each of which is given an opportunity to get the first choice of the available trafficking victims. Everyone else will have to wait until the following days to make their purchases and compete."

Ashton leaned back, partially impressed at just how intricate this whole operation was. However, it was time to show Casey that he wasn't quite as foolish as he seemed.

"You two know an awful lot about this," he said. "Just how did you manage to infiltrate Black Rose so deeply?"

It was interesting, reflecting on the details they'd given so far and noticing just how many details of their personal involvement had been omitted. Certainly, John and Miranda had provided a lot of information, but there was really only one way they could have obtained some of this information: by going deep undercover for a long, long time. Either that or working for them and this all being a lie.

"You're right to be suspicious," Miranda said, bleakly looking into her glass. "You would be poor choices for this mission otherwise. My husband and I have been working our way deeper and deeper into the confidences of human trafficking rings for nearly a decade. We never got burned when working with previous groups, so it was fairly easy for us to get recommended to Black Rose when they began their ascension to supremacy a couple of years back."

"You have to do some pretty dark things when you're undercover for that long," Casey said, her voice sounding a tad hollow.

Everyone let that statement marinate, but Ashton felt like the odd man out. It was something that the other three could relate to on a level that scarred their souls, but he didn't have that excuse for the shit that he'd done in the past. The sins that he'd committed had been on him and him alone, not in service of anything greater.

It had been a gradual change, and he hadn't even been entirely aware of it happening, but Ashton realized that the two looked remarkably different to him than they had before. They looked tired and old beyond their years, and even though the sum total of alcohol consumed between the two was a single glass of wine, it felt like they'd just finished an entire bottle of spirits together. They were wrinkled by the work that they'd done, worn down by stress and the heavy burdens on their souls.

Ashton exchanged a look with Casey. He could see the message in her eyes: don't let your guard down.

He cleared his throat. "You said something about proof, John?"

The purported British agent shuddered and returned from what was surely a brutal bit of reminiscence. "Right, I did say I would get that for you. Just a moment."

John rose to his feet, then hurried from the room.

Ashton's gaze followed him. If the man was going to leave their sight, things might get a little tricky. It would feel rude to explicitly say that he needed to keep an eye on the man so that he didn't rush off to call security, but fortunately, his destination seemed to be a briefcase that was clearly visible.

It only took the man a moment to retrieve what he needed, then he was back at the table, spreading out a series of documents ranging from personnel files to dossiers on members of Black Rose.

Casey immediately began to peruse the papers, flicking through them with blinding speed. Her eyes scanned, and her face held no expression at all.

Ashton would have broken the tension by saying something, but he had no idea what to say. And if anything, the other pair seemed satisfied with this level of suspicion.

"Seems to be in order," Casey said under her breath as she flipped through the last few pages. When she glanced up at John and Miranda, there was one last suspicious glint in her eyes, but then it faded away as she sighed.

Releasing a breath that he hadn't known he was holding, Ashton allowed himself to feel hope for the first time since they'd arrived. With allies, maybe they did have a way forward.

"And tomorrow, will there be any of the trafficking victims present for the auction? Will they be transported over to the main house?" Casey asked.

John and Miranda both looked contemplative, but they were also undeniably relieved that Casey seemed to be trusting them.

"I'm not quite sure," he said. "It's possible that they might bring over a few just for the sake of demonstration, but they might also want to keep them separated from the buyers until it's time. One thing that definitely won't happen is the transportation of all the victims over here tomorrow. I doubt that Black Rose would be so foolish as to risk something like that."

"I see," Casey said. "This may be a long night. Shall we have some coffee?"

Chapter 11

Sure enough, the conversation had lasted long into the night, starting with a breakdown of all the details that they knew for sure but eventually devolving into more companionable discussion and the sharing of anecdotes. Even though it may have seemed like they were straying from their objective, that couldn't have been further from the truth. In fact, it had been a complicated series of tests as they tried to see if they could poke holes in one another's story.

When Casey and Ashton had finally stumbled back to their room a bit past midnight, they'd been simultaneously wired and exhausted. There was so much to do, yet nothing that they could accomplish. Any plans to investigate their surroundings would have to wait until they devised a plan to infiltrate security and deal with their thermal technology.

Veronica also hadn't shown up at the room, which Casey only remembered in the morning. It would have been quite unfortunate if they'd returned in such a state to find that they then needed to thoroughly question a girl to determine if she could help them in their infiltration.

But the most shocking thing of all, Casey reflected as she paced in their room, was that she had woken up wrapped in what might even have been considered an affection embrace with Ashton. They'd barely managed to shed their clothes and had then collapsed into bed, at which point they had gotten entangled overnight.

She shivered, not so much at the fact that it had happened then at how she yearned for that to be repeated in the future. That was one complication that she could not afford.

Pausing, Casey wondered if Ashton had been successful in his mission. Without any chance of being able to sneak around, they had decided that blundering around like idiots would be the only way to get an idea of the place's layout. He had left more than an hour ago, still firmly in the middle of the morning, and had set out to ostensibly find some breakfast. Black Rose couldn't blame him too much for that other than send him back to her room.

They had decided not to revisit the British agents today until the masquerade/auction. It would be suspicious if they got too chummy, and it could even lead to all four of their covers being blown.

Should she go out and do a little boundary-pushing of her own? That was the exact question gripping her when she heard a timid knock on her door.

It was so surprising that she didn't even bother to ready her gun. It was impossible to imagine any armed goons knocking so softly.

When she opened the door, she found none other than the maid from last night. Her eyes focused intently on her own feet.

"Veronica!" Casey said, then caught just how enthusiastic she sounded. Putting on a frown for the benefit of anyone hidden and watching in the corridor, she hurriedly beckoned the girl inward. "Get in here, girl. You took your sweet time!"

It was heartbreaking how the girl flinched at the command. At least Casey could take solace in the fact that the girl's worst fears were not going to come true, not in this room.

Thanks to a more thorough sweep this morning, she was confident that there were absolutely no functional listening devices in the vicinity, so she had no second thoughts about guiding the girl to a couch and taking the seat across from her.

"Are you alright, Veronica?"

The girl looked up, blinking in confusion. There was only the faintest wetness at the corners of her eyes, but Casey got the impression that she was making a herculean effort to hold back the tide.

"Sorry, I was putting on a show for anyone listening," Casey explained before she could even consider whether that was a good idea. Something about the girl just made her want to comfort the poor thing.

By Veronica's expression, she didn't understand what Casey meant.

"If they saw that I was being too kind to you...."

"Oh," Veronica said bleakly, then she looked down at the floor once more. Her tiny shoulders sagged as she considered precisely what might be done to her if they thought she was being treated kindly.

"But we're not going to hurt you," Casey explained. "We just wanted to talk with you a bit."

"We?" Veronica glanced around, more a honed survival instinct than innocent curiosity.

"Yes, me and Adam. The man with me last night."

The girl swallowed, but at least she didn't seem terrified at the thought. "Then you're... you're not here to...."

"No, nothing like that," Casey cut in. She reached over to grab the girl's hand but thought better of it. No need to push things too hard, too fast.

By the way that Veronica was glancing around, she clearly still thought that it was a trap. Her lips were white as she forced them not to tremble.

"How old are you, dear?" Casey asked, softening her voice. Coming across as comforting to young women was never something she had practiced for. Seducing men was far more in her wheelhouse, but she was nothing if not adaptable when the mission called for it.

"F-fourteen."

The agent closed her eyes and silently counted to five. When she opened them, she tried to grip tightly to her professionalism. As strong as the urge was to give the poor lass a big hug, bigger things were at stake.

"And where are you from, Veronica? Where did they take you from?"

Her eyes widened. "I'm... I'm from here. I'm a local."

Casey fixed her with a level stare. The girl was truly a terrible liar.

"New York," the girl said as she averted her gaze, just a hint of an accent showing. "They said they were hiring models."

It was a brutally effective tactic, and it was utterly unsurprising that it had been applied here. If you want to lure a lonely teenage girl away from any support that she might have, then what better strategy than to promise her that she is beautiful and has a bright future in modeling or acting?

"How long ago was this?" Casey asked softly.

"A year ago," Veronica said, hanging her head to hide her tears, but her voice was raw with emotion.

Without a word, Casey rose and went to sit beside Veronica. She offered nothing more than an arm around her shoulder at first, giving the girl a chance to lean into the embrace or push her away. It took a moment, but silent sobs began to wrack the girl, and she turned to accept the comfort that Casey was offering.

Seconds stretched out into minutes as the girl cried, never uttering so much as a whimper. The only sound was the gentle rubbing of Casey's hand on Veronica's back. It was dangerous to allow herself to be swayed so much when the mission was on the line, but at the same time, she could feel a surging, frothing tide of rage within herself. She had hardly needed more motivation to take down Black Rose, but sometimes, that little extra push was what it took to make the truly difficult choices.

"Do you..." Casey trailed off. This would be the hard part, and she had to get it just right. Coaxing information out of someone so young would be hard, and that wasn't even accounting for the fact that the girl might actually be a plant sent by Black Rose.

But she had to take a chance at some point, and Casey simply couldn't imagine that this girl was working for a bunch of slavers.

"Do you know where the others are being kept?" Casey asked softly so that not even a physical eavesdropper at the door would be able to hear.

Veronica paused in her silent crying, pulling away and wiping her red, puffy eyes. "You mean the other maids?"

"I mean all the other girls that are here against their will. The ones that are going to be sold in the coming days?"

Veronica's eyes widened, and suddenly Casey was quite sure she had miscalculated. This girl had no idea that there would be an auction in the coming days and that knowledge could make her panic.

"Sold? People are going to be sold?"

A long, tense moment dragged out, and Casey could see the exact thoughts flashing through the girl's mind. She'd thought that she would be used and abused like this for the foreseeable future, but now she was coming to terms with the fact that she could get sent home with some of the guests, and heaven only knew how reprehensible they had been to her.

"Others," Veronica mouthed, so stricken that she couldn't even cry. "That must be what they're doing with those buildings they brought in a couple of days ago. There were big delivery trucks, but the other maids thought they were just bringing stuff for the upcoming festivities."

Well, that was one thing confirmed, at least. It wouldn't do much good until they were able to close the distance to the prefabricated complex, but it was something.

"Do you want anything to eat or drink?" Casey asked, almost reflexively. The girl looked so stricken and emotionally charged that a little nourishment would be sure to do her good.

"I can't," Veronica said in an instant, but her body language was much less convincing. Her eyes darted over to the largely untouched breakfast still sitting on a table after having been brought by other servants earlier.

"You can," Casey reassured her. Then, to drive home the point, she got up, went and picked up the tray, and brought it back for the girl.

The meal had been large enough for two, but neither had taken more than a small bite, so there was an overwhelming pile of leftovers. Half a dozen scrambled eggs, a heaping portion of hash browns, two cups of fruit, another half-dozen pieces of toast, and a small selection of bacon, sausage, and ham reflected in the maid's eyes.

It took very little more to convince the poor girl to eat. Soon enough, she was chowing down like she hadn't had a decent meal in the last week. If Casey's suspicions were correct, it had probably been a lot longer than that.

For a long moment, the agent merely sat and listened to the ravenous sounds beside her, allowing her festering hate to boil down and crystallize into something more useful. Soon enough, there was nothing but a lump at the bottom of her belly, a brutal determination that she would do whatever was necessary to save this girl and every other girl like her. Sometimes, that cold certainty made the difference when it came to pulling the trigger and ending a life in an instant. On this mission, there would be no hesitation whatsoever, no quiet moments of contemplation when she wondered if the simple henchmen of Black Rose deserved death for being in her way.

"Do you have any family that we can get you back to?" Casey asked softly.

At first, Veronica gave no sign of having heard. She shoveled another spoonful of eggs into her mouth, then washed it down with a greedy gulp of orange juice.

"No, there's nobody," she said quickly. Too quickly.

But Casey wasn't going to pry. If the girl did have family, she probably thought that she was too ruined to be sent back to them, and that went double if she'd had some sort of sweetheart back wherever she came from. It was going to be a sensitive conversation when they finally did have it, but it had no bearing on the mission at hand for now.

Unfortunately, it was at that exact moment that Ashton returned from his mission. He opened the door cautiously, but he was on the lookout for any ambushes, not the presence of a maid sitting on his couch and eating his breakfast. Naturally, he pieced together the situation fairly quickly, but not before she spotted him and her eyes widened to a new record.

Only Casey's quick reflexes managed to get a hand clamped over the girl's mouth before she could yelp in surprise.

"Don't worry, he's here to help," Casey said hastily, trying to be as soothing as possible but not sure that was coming across at all.

She could feel Veronica shaking beneath her hand, but as she tentatively let the girl go, she was relieved to see that she wouldn't immediately scream out for help.

"We're going to help you get out of here," Casey said quietly, patting the poor girl's back. "You just have to hang in there a bit longer. Can you do that?"

Ashton looked to his partner. "Does she have any information we can use?" It wasn't exactly the most sensitive thing that he could have said, but at least it wasn't a flippant joke like she had half-feared.

"I don't think so," Veronica said. Now that the adrenaline was fading, joining the emotional exhaustion and the massive amount of food that she'd just consumed, the girl seemed to deflate before their eyes. "I don't think I know enough to be of any real help, and if you two get caught, then I will feel terrible and like it was my fault."

Casey and Ashton exchanged a glance, and then he moved to take a seat on the other side of Veronica.

Chapter 12

It took a little under half an hour for them to console Victoria, ensure that she wasn't going to talk to anyone else, clean her up, and send her on her merry way. When she finally did depart, her eyes were still red, but Casey assured Ashton that it wouldn't be remarked upon too much. If anything, her superiors would simply assume that she was treated exactly as they'd intended. They'd briefly considered allowing her to stay in their room, but odds were extremely high that their quarters would be searched in their absence.

More and more, Ashton found himself closing his eyes and steadying his breathing. It was getting harder and harder to fight the urge to go to their luggage, unlock the trick compartment in the bottom, and arm himself to the teeth with the implements of death found there. Only his tenuous hold on the vague notion of a greater good kept him from going on a killing spree at the earliest convenience.

But it was good to get these bloody thoughts out of the way before the big event, he reasoned. Better to come to terms with them before he actually had to face down however many sick bastards he was going to have to smile at tonight. And sick bitches, he conceded. If last night had told him anything, it was that women could be just as reprehensible when it came to trafficking in human flesh.

Without knowing when they would be summoned to the "surprise" masquerade, there wasn't much to do aside from sit tight and wait. They'd already selected exactly what they were going to wear, and he found himself imagining just how it would feel to help Casey strip out of her clothing and change. It was enough to make his blood run hot, and he had to avert his gaze so as to not raise her ire.

"What is it?" she grumbled as he paced across the room once more.

Ashton glanced back at her. He meant it to be nothing more than a quirk of an eyebrow, but the vexation lining her face did terrible things to his core. She looked so imperious, sitting in her chair with a painfully straight back and watching him without turning her head. He knew in his head that it was just a matter of getting into character for the evening, but his other head was of a very different opinion.

He had to flex his hands just to distract himself, but that also drew her attention as well. Maybe it was just his imagination, but he thought he saw her pupils dilate fractionally as she looked at those tensing fingers. What was she thinking of at this moment? Him gripping her tightly? Her wrists, her waist, or something a little more vulnerable?

Ashton stepped closer to her, purely by instinct alone. Her lips parted ever so slightly, and she tilted her head back just enough that he knew his mind wasn't playing tricks on him. Looking down at her, it was easy to take in every little curve and swell of her body, every place that he knew his hands fit perfectly. They were made for one another, and he vowed that he was going to show her that one last time when this mission was over. If she wanted nothing to do with him after that, then so be it, but he would get to make his final argument to her primal side.

Of course, that's exactly the moment when a sharp rap sounded on the door, which made both of them jump slightly.

For a moment, the pair simply blinked and looked at one another, followed promptly by a couple of sheepish grins. Smoothing their features, she adjusted herself to sit just a little more imperiously, and he went to the door.

Opening it just a crack, he found one of the guards that he'd noticed before. A square, blockish fellow with a nose that had been broken too many times to count, Ashton had instantly disliked. Things hadn't improved when the agent had been sneaking around this morning and overheard this man and several other hired goons bragging about their exploits with women. Ordinarily, that wasn't particularly noteworthy, but when the only available options nearby were implicitly unwilling at best...

"Can I help you?" Ashton murmured..

Those beady little eyes looked him up and down, practically screaming his inner thoughts. The bastard was probably interpreting his state of relative undress as a consequence of having been interrupted in the middle of relations. It was annoying enough to have the pig thinking of Casey being fucked, but it was even more annoying that Ashton hadn't been making her moan and scream with pleasure.

Suddenly, the guard remembered why he'd been sent and his brow furrowed. "That's right, I'm here to inform you that there's to be a large event tonight. Our hosts politely request that you attend."

Which meant that attendance was mandatory.

"Very well, we'll get ready and then make our way there. I assume that a servant will guide us?" Ashton asked, adding an edge of irritation to his tone.

"Nah, I'll just wait here," the guard said with a leering smile, his eyes flicking past Ashton as if he could actually see anything further in the room. It was clear that he wanted to listen to any further sounds that might come from the inhabitants of the room resuming whatever activities he'd imagined them to be in the midst of when interrupted.

Snorting, Ashton shut the door and turned back to Casey, who looked positively regal, even in little more than a nightgown.

"Let's get ready," he said, certain that every word was being listened to. No sense in saying anything that might compromise them.

"Yes, let's," Casey replied. Besides, there was no need for words when their locked eyes told every word of the story. They'd gone over their plans, now all that was left was the execution and a test of just how flexible they could be in the face of operational difficulties.

It only took a matter of moments for them to don the outfits that they'd selected. While dressing in advance had been an option, it may have raised some suspicions if the guards noticed that they were ready for an event before even being told that it was happening. They were new buyers, and were thus expected to be blindsided by most happenings.

By necessity, they helped one another. Casey straightened his tie while he adjusted her bustline, ensuring that it showed as much as possible without actually being in danger of slipping off. He felt a surge of desire at the touch of her skin in such a sensitive, erotic place, then another surge as he imagined other men (and women) looking at her with the desire that her attire was meant to cultivate. The jealousy must have shown all over his face because Casey was half-way smirking at him when they separated and evaluated their handiwork from a few steps away.

"Hopefully nobody gets too handsy," he remarked.

"Hopefully not," she agreed, and even the playful note in their banter was undercut by their shared contemplation of darker ramifications. They were at the mercy of the enemy here. Being handsy could be more than just a drunken guest wanting to cop a feel. There could be some very big players here with very broad expectations of what they should be allowed to do to women.

Once they were ready, they put on perfected expressions of bored indolence and swept out into the hallway. They were immediately greeted by a pair of guards, one of which was the fellow that Ashton had spoken with before. There was not a maid in sight. It would seem that they were being told in no uncertain terms that they were not to wander.

The naked lust that was immediately directed towards Casey sent a chilling reminder down Ashton's spine. She really was a beautiful woman, almost inhumanly so. With the vibrant makeup that she'd applied, all it would take was one flutter of her eyelashes to reduce a man to a slavery mess. Suddenly, he understood perfectly why she hadn't decided to go all out on dressing up for actual evenings out in the past. To her, getting made up and making the most of her assets was associated with work and all the heavy baggage that came with that.

They were escorted down into a wing that he hadn't been able to scout at all during his earlier forays. Every time that he'd stumbled in this general direction, he'd been physically blocked from progressing any further by guards just like these.

However, his early reconnaissance hadn't been completely fruitless. It had imparted upon him an understanding of how truly labyrinthine the estate was, and so he didn't wonder why they hadn't run into any other guests heading in the same direction as they were escorted. If his intuition was correct, then various guests were being led along different routes, never to intersect until they actually reached the ballroom. This would be repeated over the course of several hours until everyone was moved.

There was very little ceremony when they finally did reach the exceptionally large double doors that must surely lead to the masquerade ball. The guards moved to open both doors at once, and Ashton felt Casey tense at his side. Her expression never wavered, but from this close distance and his extensive experience in studying her face up close, he could see the tension at the corners of her eyes.

"Ah right, you'll be needing these," the more irritating of the two guards said, fishing around in his coat pocket and pulling out a pair of silver masquerade masks. They were largely unadorned, and Ashton immediately wondered if the specific color was a marking for what class of guest they were.

"Thank you," Ashton said as he took the pair, first placing a mask upon his mistress's face before tending to his own needs. The grazing of his fingers upon her ears was so fleeting that it may as well never have happened, yet he felt the slight puff of air as she breathed out. It was little comfort, but maybe he had alleviated just a tiny bit of her anxiety. If they were going to get through this, then he needed her to be in top form.

When he stepped back and peered out through the holes on his own mask, he was caught by just how dangerously mysterious Casey looked. There was little else that could be read in her face, so he had to draw even greater meaning from her eyes, and what he saw was so devastatingly alluring that he could already imagine pulling this familiar stranger into a side room and having his way with her. If there weren't going to be a thousand trysts in the masquerade ball, then he was going to be very shocked.

There was some small solace to be had though. As they straightened out and waited for the guards to actually open the doors, he wondered if he must also look so mysterious and enticing. If so, maybe he could actually extract some information from the other women, like that Erika woman from before.

The doors opened, and the utter silence gave way to the susurration of a classy party involving nothing but strangers. The room before them was massive, an old ballroom that must have been built years and years ago, converted to accommodate more modern forms of high class celebrations. There were no tables of food lining the walls, but rather servants that carried trays in endless patterns, weaving between groups of sophisticated, elegant slavers that showed not a single speck of their twisted motives in how they chattered about art, the weather, and the economy.

When the pair stepped into the room, nobody turned to notice them. Casey glanced back to check if the guards were following. They were not, and had already begun to close the doors, surely about to go escort the next set of guests in.

"Just as we planned," Casey murmured under her breath. "Let's split up for now."

Ashton nodded at that, scanning the crowd for any familiar faces. Most masks were silver, like theirs, but some were gold and other shades of metal. The servants appeared to be wearing bronze. The British agents would be a welcome sight, but he'd have to figure out a way to approach them naturally. Until that point, he would need to ingratiate himself with some other groups.

Lo and behold, he spotted the fiery redhead from last night, cackling to a horde of men that were hanging onto every word. She was wearing a scandalous dress that made Casey look downright conservative, along with a golden mask that perched precariously on her nose. All the men around her wore silver.

A shared glance with Casey confirmed that they were of one mind on this. He thought he caught a glimpse of regret in her eyes, but then it was gone, and she was going her own way. Well, if she was being tormented by the thought of him being with another woman, then he sure wasn't going to make things worse for himself by looking to see what man she was on her way to beguile.

And then there was nothing on Ashton's mind but how to coax answers from the woman before him. In fact, he was no longer even Ashton Malick at all. Now, there was only Adam Johnson.

Erika was the first to notice him, but she acted like she didn't. In the middle of listening to what was surely a lazy and uninspired quip, her eyes ran up and down his body, showing neither approval nor disapproval, then she turned back to the simpering sycophant at her side, laughing just a little too forcefully. They all watched her with absolute adoration, eager that she might throw them table scraps. They were all so polite too, never daring to look at anything but her face, never showing a single sign that what they really wanted was to fuck her senseless.

Good, that made things easy for Ashton. All he had to do was give her something a little different.

"We meet again," he drawled as he stepped closer, flicking a hand before a passing servant and snagging a pair of champagne flutes. "What was it? Erika?"

She tilted her head to regard him, and the half dozen men around her snapped around, incensed at this lack of respect. Who was he to treat their prize with such familiarity and disrespect?

"It was," she said, her voice sultry and smokey. A good choice for wrapping men around her finger, that was for certain. "And you were... Adam?"

"At your service," he said with a lazy grin, sweeping his gaze across her fawning followers. "If I didn't know any better, I would say that you were going to tire yourself out in the bedroom tonight."

Casey had relayed all of the pertinent details about the woman's idea of bedsport, and by the amusement on Erika's face, she had been completely correct.

Of course, all the gathered men instantly turned a remarkable shade of red and looked about ready to get into a fistfight on the spot. There wasn't even a point in distinguishing between them, not when they were all so clearly disposable fonts of praise and perhaps overenthusiastic cunnilingus.

"And does Eve know you're here?" Erika asked before any of them could do anything regrettable.

A tricky question. Would this woman be more interested if he said no, suggesting that this was a matter of cheating and betrayal, or yes, suggesting that there was a mutual understanding or open relationship. Given where they were and why they were here, the decision seemed obvious.

"No, she's distracted with business."

Erika looked like a cat who had gotten into the milk, and he could practically see her skin flush with excitement. It really was too easy to read her.

Ashton looked over the foolish men once more, this time letting his gaze linger on each. One wore glasses, another didn't. One had shaved hair, another long. None of it mattered, he wasn't even paying attention to them so much as he was showing just how little he cared about the men who would claim to have been here first.

"You look bored here. Would you like to change that?" he asked, turning his attention back to Erika and making sure that everyone watched as he took in her beyond plunging neckline, the way that her dress was clinging to her hips for dear life, and even the barely-visible outline of her womanhood. Oh yes, this woman was being comically blatant with her sexuality, and all the men around her thought that it would be rude to remark on it.

One man stepped forward, his fist trembling at his side. He was on the shorter side, but that didn't mean that he was completely harmless.

In the blink of an eye, Ashton stepped past him, brushing him lightly to the side as if he was just an annoying bit of fabric. And then, there was nobody closer to Erika than him.

If he was right, then these men weren't willing to make an actual scene here. If any of them were truly high enough on the pecking order to have him dragged off and beaten to death, then there was no way that they would be simpering like this.

The would-be gallant knight's face had crumpled as he stepped out of the way, but when Erika looked up at him, she was practically trembling. In that instant, everything that he'd suspected was confirmed. She was a spoiled little princess that wanted to know what it was like for a man to take what he wanted from her. Good, that was easy enough to provide.

Before she could even react, he pushed a flute of champagne into her hand, then reached up and flicked the corner of her golden mask. It fell from her face, revealing a shocked expression as the poor woman struggled to process what was even happening to her. She'd wanted an impudent man, but she was about to find out what it was really like to lose control.

"Oh dear, it looks like you dropped your mask. Let's find somewhere a little more private and put it back on," Ashton said, his voice low and projecting just enough so that everyone around could hear. They too were stunned at his arrogance and unable to do more than gasp.

Erika nodded, her body clearly racing ahead of her mind. And then, in his most daring move yet, Ashton linked his arm through hers, and gently guided her away from the center of the festivities, leaving her mask on the ground. He could not possibly have been any clearer in his intentions, not to her, not to her little pawns, not to anyone that had been watching.

Chapter 13

Casey kept an eye on Ashton, pleased with his performance. There was no room for personal feelings here, only the cold ruthlessness required to complete the mission.

For her part, she made a slow circuit around the room's perimeter, noting as much as she could about the number of people, how many people there were with each kind of mask, how many exits there were, and anything suspicious that might be going on. All told, there were more than two hundred people in the room, but the vast majority were either guests wearing silver or servants wearing bronze. That substantially cut down the number of people that she needed to investigate.

She was still undecided about whether to approach any of the guests wearing gold masks. That would be one of the fastest ways to get herself into the secret auction later, but at the same time, it would also be the quickest way to get caught if things went south.

Over the course of the evening, she'd noted almost all of the guests that had been present in the Brits' apartment earlier. Erika was being seduced by Ashton, Olya was engaged in a heated discussion about geopolitics with some burly fellows in one of the corners, and the British agents had split up just like Casey and Ashton.

The only one that she couldn't quite find was the man with the nasty cough. Now that she thought about it, she'd never actually learned his name, had she? She'd have to remember to ask John or Miranda about that later.

"Speak of the devil," Casey muttered under her breath, for who was cutting across the room in her direction but Miranda? Although, after a moment's consideration, it appeared that the woman was in somewhat of a hurry. She was trying to hide it, but she was most certainly exerting herself.

How odd, and by odd, she meant deeply worrying.

Casey scanned the room as surreptitiously as she could, but it didn't look like anyone was paying them too much attention.

"Miranda?"

"We don't have much—" the woman began, but her voice cut off as she snapped her mouth shut. The way her eyes widened as she looked past Casey could only mean one thing.

Bracing herself, the agent schooled her face to boredom and turned around, coming face to face with a man wearing a black mask. Unlike all the others, this one didn't just simply cover up the eyes and above the nose. This was fitted to every contour of his face, painting a grim and foreboding portrait of a man, and he was most certainly looking down on her.

"Eve Johnson, I take it? And hello, Miranda." His voice rumbled like gravel, grating on Casey's very soul.

"That is correct, but I'm afraid you have me at a disadvantage here," Casey said, daring a glance over at Miranda. To her credit, the woman didn't look flustered at all and had recovered that calm austerity that she had exuded during their first meeting with Erika and Olya.

His eyes burned into hers as if he was searching his very soul, but he said nothing at all to her implied question.

"This is the woman, Miranda?" For the first time, Casey realized just how remarkably intimidating the man was. He wasn't particularly broad, nor was he overwhelmingly tall or muscled, thus it was quite the testament to his sheer presence and bearing that he could feel so utterly massive compared to her, drowning out the entire rest of the world.

This was the master of Black Rose. It simply had to be.

"And good, you found her partner," he mused.

Ashton approached, John beside him. All four agents now stood before one of the most dangerous men in the world, and nobody around was paying any attention. Had they been betrayed? Was this all a setup?

Casey forced herself to think logically. Even if Miranda and John had orchestrated this, then there was nothing that they could do right now. Any attempt to fight back or flee would result in them being killed or worse, and the captives being whisked away, never to be seen again. Even if their mission here failed and they were caught, then the bureau might still be able to pull something off.

And yet Casey wasn't quite sure they had been betrayed, not yet.

"You are sure that they would be suitable candidates for the auction?" the master of Black Rose asked.

John nodded. "Yes, they mentioned being on the fence about the merchandise before, but I think they can be easily persuaded with a little demonstration."

Casey held her breath, and she could practically feel Ashton doing the same. They really might get to see the auction without having to sneak their way in. This had gone from being unspeakable bad luck to the best of fortune in the blink of an eye.

In the silence that followed, she was able to take in every little nuance of their strange configuration. The master loomed, confident in his power. Ashton was torn between bristling at the man who challenged him on every level, from the moral and the spiritual to the physical. John and Miranda watched with a quiet tension, surely born of their fear that this ruse would be discovered but easily masked beneath the lie that they just wanted the master to look favorably upon their proposal. And Casey could only hope that she was

"Perhaps it could be entertaining," the master said after what sounded like an eternity. "And I would be most interested to hear their advice on what I should purchase."

Casey bit her tongue. Should she play the awestruck fool, unwilling to dare anything that might risk such a man's ire, or should she try to act haughty and use that to glean a tiny bit more information? In the end, the temptation was simply too much.

"What would you need to buy? I thought you owned everything here."

For a moment, she feared that she had made a grave mistake. There was absolutely no reaction on his face as he stared into her, not to begin with.

And then, although she could see nothing of his lips beneath that terrible mask, she could still make out the gleam of humor in his eyes.

"True, I have no need to purchase anything for professional reasons. However, I will be attending the auction for personal pleasure, and I assure you that the pleasure will be very personal."

Nothing changed in his eyes, not a single thing. As he insinuated that he was going to be abusing slaves for his own amusement, he kept that same bemused humor that she had inspired with her overeager questioning.

Casey couldn't remember the last time she'd met someone that so thoroughly chilled her to the bone.

But she had to play her part, so in spite of the chill running up and down her spine, she politely chuckled along with the other three agents.

"And what about you?" the master asked as he turned to Ashton. Even though they were of a height, the difference between them seemed impossible. "What kind of... merchandise are you planning to purchase? Will any be for personal usage?"

Deep down, in her heart of hearts, Casey prayed more than she'd ever prayed for anything in her life. Let Ashton play it cool. Let him not give in to anger and say something flippant. If she could have shut her eyes without it being obvious and noteworthy, then she would have done so.

After a fraction of a second, Ashton laughed. It was harsh and woefully lacking in authenticity, but hopefully, she only recognized that because she'd heard so many of his genuine, mirthful laughs.

"If there are any girls that strike my fancy, then I certainly shall indulge. Just one or two shouldn't annoy Eve too much."

Casey felt sick to her stomach, but she rolled her eyes extravagantly. "Just remember that for every one little chit you get, I get two men. That was the deal."

A sensible chuckle was shared by all, and Casey couldn't help but wonder how Miranda and John managed. How could you be around people that enjoyed this sort of thing for years on end? How could you go along with it, laughing like it wasn't the most profane thing you could ever even begin to imagine?

But there they were, smiling politely and visibly growing less tense as the master of Black Rose accepted the two that they had brought. Casey could only hope that she would be half as skilled as them when she was their age.

"Firm rules are the bedrock of any stable relationship," Miranda said, raising her wine.

"Hear, hear," John agreed with a chortle, clinking their glasses together.

It was the slightest thing. Nothing more than a casual look at each of the four people before him, but there was something deeply unsettling about the way that the master's gaze lingered. Perhaps it was just Casey's imagination, but she still had to fight down the urge to step back and flee.

A great bell tolled, echoing all around.

"Ah, good, it is time for the auction. Let us go," the master said. This time, it was definitely not Casey's imagination. He most certainly looked her in the eye and had something disturbing on his mind.

Chapter 14

It was terrifying in its mundanity. That was the only way Ashton could manage to think of the hour that followed. A number of men and women filed into a side chamber with an elevated stage at the front. Everyone continued to stand and mill about in small groups, and servers continued to deliver a continuous stream of refreshments. And, from time to time, the masked man standing upon the stage would direct their attention to a new projected image of a piece of art being displayed. A vase here, a painting there, always being ostensibly shown beside a woman that was invariably trying to mask sheer terror behind a rictus smile. The crowd would chatter amongst themselves, and a few hands would be raised. Notes would be taken, and then everything moved along to the next piece of human flesh on display.

Their little group of five swelled and diminished as various other men and women wandered by to pay their respects to the master, complimenting him on the success of the evening. He accepted them all graciously, acting as if this was nothing more than a typical house party for the fabulously wealthy.

While the mission may have benefited greatly from the fact that the master of Black Rose desired their continued company during the affair, that didn't make it any easier to bear, if anything, the thought that the man approved of them just made him feel even more vile.

Ashton watched as yet another image was displayed for the whole room to see. There was practically no ceremony about it, just an antique ceramic vessel held by a woman who couldn't have been any older than Veronica. It was like her pleading eyes were reaching out to him and him alone. Before he could shatter the glass in his hand, he downed the bitterest of wines and haphazardly tossed it onto the tray of a passing servant.

The master of Black Rose watched this whole exchange and said nothing, but there was no sign of disapproval in his gaze. It sickened Ashton to think that the man approved of such flippant disregard for the inhuman cruelty going on around him.

There was no sign of the actual victims though, not in this room. In a sense, that did give them a little more information to go on. After all, if they weren't going to bring out actual samples for this, then they wouldn't have brought them out for anything. They were likely still secured in the complex of prefabricated buildings, so if one of them could just get over there and orchestrate some sort of breakout...

It was almost hypnotizing, in a way. Ashton found himself watching the people all around with nihilistic amusement. There was nothing else to do, and so he found himself wondering what had led each and every one of these individuals to be in such a place as this, lazily inspecting men and women to purchase for their own amusement?

Did any of them have a single justifiable reason to be here? Some sort of brutal lifelong trauma, perhaps inflicted upon them because they were a slave like this in the past, something that drove them to pathologically continue the cycle? Or would it be an unquestionable good for every person here wearing gold or silver masks to just die on the spot. It was a rhetorical question right up until he wondered if it might be necessary to destroy the entire place and kill everyone in it.

But no, that couldn't happen so long as there were servants like Veronica present. Some of the guards were probably victims in their own ways as well.

With a sigh, Ashton turned his attention back to the lull in the conversation beside him. An older group of men that almost definitely worked in finance had just finished lavishing the master with praise, but their departure had left a void, and so Ashton found himself inadvertently locking eyes with the man himself.

"I have a proposal if you're interested," the master said smoothly, his stare never wavering.

"Yes?"

The master looked over at Casey, John, and Miranda, who were only a few feet away, but were engrossed in utterly inconsequential conversation with a woman that spoke with a thick Chinese accent.

"In exchange, I would provide you with a taste of the merchandise, in private and ahead of schedule."

"In exchange for what?" Ashton asked, but his mouth was drier than hell. This could be the break they were waiting for. If he was escorted to see the victims, then he could surely figure out a way to infiltrate later, or maybe he could even pass a message along to some of them. If they knew that help was coming, they could be ready to break out the moment they put their plan into motion. Eliminating crucial minutes and seconds of confusion and hesitation would be imperative to accomplishing their goals.

He was already so far gone in visualizing the bounty of his rewards that he had scarcely given a thought to what was needed in exchange, but that changed the instant that the master opened his mouth once more.

"The older couple that you've befriended... I want to see them brought down a peg."

Ashton remained silent, watching the only other people in this place that he even vaguely trusted, and wondered if they could hear any of this. They were truly great actors, but even they would surely react to hearing this.

"Down a peg?" he repeated his voice nearly a whisper.

"Yes," the master whispered right back as he leaned in just enough that Ashton could hear the mask vibrating with his voice. "I want to see you with her and your partner with him. It would amuse me."

Ashton blinked, certain that he must have misheard something there. But the master continued, utterly inexorable.

"You see, I enjoy watching how people fit together. I like to throw disparate groups into rooms and see what happens, whether it be copulation or homicide. In the past, I've thrown John and Miranda into a number of... difficult situations, for that is a natural consequence of spending enough time around the Black Rose. Interestingly, what seems to affect them most is watching one another be used down to the last drop."

"W-why?" Ashton couldn't help but ask. Sweat beaded beneath the mask, and he could already feel a combination of revulsion and arousal swirling in his gut. Over the course of their brief time together, he'd slowly realized that Miranda was quite an attractive woman, but the circumstances were beyond horrific. Every one of his little appreciative glances now felt like a brutal betrayal.

"Because it pleases me," the master said, and not a word more.

Ashton was thankful for the lengthening moment of silence as both watched the other group. The masks made it easy to hide exactly where your attention was unless someone was paying close attention to your eyes.

"If Casey agrees," he said softly, but he knew that it was already a foregone conclusion. In that instant, he could already envision her giving herself entirely to the mission, fucking John like an animal and shattering any relationships in her way. After all, it was simply collateral damage in the course of achieving the greater good.

"Artemis, Gerald." The master's tone was nothing more than conversational, but both visibly winced as they turned to look at him. How many times had they been through this before that they could already recognize what he was about to say?

It was a tiny thing, almost imperceptible, but after turning to give the master their attention, John ended up putting himself a little in front of his wife as if to protect her from the master's cruel designs. Ashton could almost feel his heart shrivel up, and he refused to look at the woman he may be bedding against her will in the near future.

"Yes, sir?" John asked, doing an admirable job of not letting his apprehension bleed through into his voice. Nevertheless, Ashton was damn sure that the master could see just how worried the man was, especially if they'd been through this song and dance before.

"I would like to indulge in a little more bedroom chemistry if you will," the master said, casually putting an arm around Ashton's shoulder. "What do you think? Both of you couples in a bedroom, the usual rules and all that."

John swallowed, and the tension of the moment was such that everyone watched his Adam's apple bob.

"The... as you wish, sir."

"Oh, cheer up, old fellow," the master said, mocking his accent. "Remember that you at least seem to like the Johnsons here. It could be so very much worse, like last time."

Miranda blanched at that, and John's jaw tensed. Just what had this bastard done to these poor people?

For the first time, Ashton dared to make eye contact with Casey. There was utter calm in her gaze, a dispassionate edge that immediately gave him a sense of relief. So she was just as pissed about this as he was. Maybe they could figure out a way to avoid this yet.

"So what do you say, Eve?" the master asked. "Your fellow here said he was fine with it as long as you went along."

"Did he now?" she asked, her voice frigid.

"Indeed, in exchange for the first crack at some of the human flesh. Poor Gerald and Artemis, being traded around so cheaply."

Suddenly, Ashton was quite sure exactly what sort of man he was dealing with. The master of Black Rose may have been scheming, but he was also overconfident and beholden to whims. He thought that he could manipulate people and that he had the power to do it however he pleased. To him, all this pain and suffering was just a way to keep entertained, and even the arm that appeared to be so casually resting across his shoulders was a tense reminder, a display of force that he wanted to be damn sure that Ashton understood.

Oh, he understood, alright. And with a quick nod to Casey, she understood as well.

"Well, why didn't you say so in the first place?" she asked, her voice sultry as she sidled up next to John and brushed her fingers down his side. "I've done a lot worse for a lot less."

Chapter 15

It was rather disturbing, Casey reflected distantly. Human beings weren't designed to do this. They weren't made for separating their bodies and minds, for stashing their emotions and souls away while their bodies endured pain and torment.

But, as she was escorted down the hallway, surrounded by three people with whom she was going to be having sex with very soon, she was able to do it nonetheless. She was able to separate her heart from the mission and prepare herself to endure whatever came next. She was a professional, and she hadn't lied before when she said that this was but a drop in the bucket compared to what she had withstood for the sake of others.

Ashton wasn't at her side. Instead, she had her arm linked through John's. Ashton was a few paces behind her, escorting Miranda in much the same way. Ahead and behind, walking so casually that they might as well have just been heading in the same general direction by circumstance, pairs of burly guards were guiding them to the rooms where they would be expected to perform.

Maybe it would be recorded, maybe not. It made no difference either way to Casey. At the very least, the other participants here were equally unwilling. Perhaps it was an unkind perspective, but sometimes that was all it took to get through the next moment: the idea that at least you weren't the one suffering the most. At least someone else was enduring even greater misery and someone who wasn't equipped quite as well as you were for this brutality. And in the end, it didn't matter whether it was kind or not because there was no room for mercy and empathy when it came to exploiting base human desires and doing whatever it took to complete the mission.

Casey stole a glance at John, disguised as peering up at him through her eyelashes. When he looked back down at her, of course, he got an eyeful of her chest as well. Everything was calculated. It always had been, it always would be.

On his face, there were all the signs of arousal. His eyes dilated ever so slightly, she could see his nostrils faintly flare as he breathed harder, and there was just the beginning of a flush on his neck. He wanted her, but even so, she could also see just how resigned he was. Between the two of them, she was clearly much better accustomed to such sacrifices.

She recognized the route they were using. In a few moments, they would be arriving at the apartments that belonged to John and Miranda. It was a sobering thought to imagine that this was the typical place used for Black Rose to torment the couple. How could one sleep in a bed normally when they had just been forced to use it to cheat on their partner and watch their partner cheat on them?

There was silence as they reached the door in question, punctuated only by the turning of a key in a lock as the guards before them cleared the way. Out of the corner of her eye, Casey wasn't quite sure, but she thought she spied Black Rose himself slipping into one of the adjacent rooms. So he wanted to watch in person, did he?

John tensed at her side as they were led in. The atmosphere was completely different from their first meeting here. Now, there was a strange sense of camaraderie between the four, whereas it had been nothing but mutual suspicion before. Casey was careful not to completely let go of her paranoia, but she couldn't help the small sense of compassion that she felt for the man at her side. If he really was an agent of the British crown, if he really was married to Miranda and deep undercover, then this must be hell.

He stole a look back at his wife. Something passed over his face, a quiet resolve, and then he turned to look down at Casey.

It wasn't being overly charitable to say that he was handsome. He had a dignified visage, and from the side, he might almost be considered regal. Casey hadn't considered his appeal in anything but the rawest and most emotionless calculations of whether she might have to sleep with the man to achieve her mission's goals, but now that he looked at her with the spark of desire and necessity, she could feel a warmth growing in her own core.

"So they really want us to do this?" she asked, not completely manufacturing the shiver in her voice.

"They do," he said gruffly.

Together, the four of them were shown the way to the bedroom, where there were two large beds already set up. It didn't look like things had been rearranged by Black Rose for this encounter. Rather, it seemed that there had always been two beds here, both perfectly made and surrounded by all the trappings of a well-lived space.

"Do you normally sleep in separate beds?" Ashton asked behind her. Was it just Casey's imagination, or could she feel his hot breath on the back of her neck?

"No," Miranda replied, and even though Casey couldn't see her face, she could feel the weight of those words. They usually slept in the same bed, but Black Rose had put another one in there so that they could always be reminded of what they had to do and how they had been debased for his amusement.

"Our host has a rather... interesting sense of humor," Casey mused, her voice dripping with sarcasm. Then, just to make sure that anyone listening didn't find that too suspicious, she began to ease one of her straps down her shoulder.

She had eyes for nobody but the man before her, the slightly older fellow who had a wife he loved and a mission he was willing to sacrifice much for. He stared back, but his eyes were inevitably drawn down to the movement of her fingers.

One bed for them, one for Ashton and Miranda. Though it felt wrong on a fundamental level to Casey, she couldn't help but imagine the sight of her own partner taking a woman right in front of her. She could practically imagine the jealous rage that he would put into every thrust, eager to make Casey suffer more than he was.

This would be an arms race of the most twisted variety imaginable. Two couples competing to see who could hurt the other more, four people racing for desire that they didn't want, all so they could put on a show and hopefully lull their tormentor into a false sense of security.

Well, never let it be said that Casey Anderson was one to back down from a challenge. There was a brutal, carnal sensuality to how she let her dress fall down to bunch at her belt. Her motions were smooth and fast, covering up any potential trembling. A push and a pull, a grabbing of the tie, and then a shoving down to the mattress, and poor John was lying on his back, staring up at her with flushed cheeks.

It was easy enough to look at him in this new light, searching for anything that might arouse her. The bones of his cheek were pronounced and tempting to touch. It was the angular sort of face that could display intensity and desire with great effect. His eyes were light and had previously been quite suited to the mild amusement he carried with himself. Now, they were dim. Averting her gaze from that depressing sight was easy enough.

Buttons fell away as she stripped his chest, demanding that his flesh made itself available. His gentle panting grew hoarser as she showed equal parts skill and flagrant disregard for his comfort. Dragging fingers down his belly, cresting the bulging outline in his pants, and caressing his inner thighs, she forced him to tense arousal. If he hadn't been hard before, he certainly was now.

It would have been a lie to say that this was one of the most terrible things that she'd ever done, but as Casey bent down and ran her tongue over his clothed crotch, she looked over and finally checked in on what the other pair was doing. That was what she told herself, anyway. In truth, it came naturally to make eye contact with the woman whose husband she was stealing away for herself.

Miranda had those same dim eyes, but they were burning just a little hotter with resentment. Ashton was making his way much slower, giving all sorts of tender affection and foreplay to the woman. Foolish man, didn't he realize that prolonging this sort of thing was anything but kindness?

Still, it didn't inhibit Casey's mission at all. In fact, she knew that he would quickly catch on once she had a mouthful of man.

"You're big," she purred for good measure, knowing that the vibrations of her mouth would travel right through the thin, rich, comfortable fabric of his pants.

"I... yes," he said, barely able to control his voice. His hips rose of their own accord, and she felt the weight of his lust. The man was inches away from abandoning all discipline and fucking her face on the spot.

Good, he knew how to make this go smoothly as well. Appeal to her instincts, make her want to drive him crazy and get the job done. That little bit of hesitance just made stripping him down to his pure desire all the more enticing.

To her surprise, when she looked over at the other bed, ready to tease the other pair of partners, she saw that Miranda already had one hand deep inside Ashton's pants. Their eyes were locked on one another, a staring contest as she stroked his cock. Neither backed down, and Casey felt the embers of jealousy ignite in her own heart.

It was a pleasant ache, stretching her boundaries that she hadn't dealt with in quite some time.

A hand pressed against her breast, not clumsily, but undoubtedly forcefully. There was no tender touching as John squeezed and tended to his own urges. Out of the corner of her eye, she could see that he too was watching the spectacle beside them.

"I think I can finish you before your wife can finish my man," she whispered.

His breath caught, but whatever retort he had primed was cut off by the unzipping of his pants. His cock straining in search of pleasure.

She could fit her fingers around it, but only barely. Her body was already responding to his provocation, anticipating what it would be like to be filled by him. It would seem that her lurid boundaries were not the only thing that would be stretched tonight.

And then, risking everything that they had worked to accomplish thus far, she leaned in even closer and nibbled on his ear. As her fingers deftly explored his shaft, she whispered so quietly that it was nearly silent.

"What's the plan?"

John twitched beneath her, but he covered it up as a spasm of pleasure. Reaching up, he grabbed the back of her head with just a touch of force, squeezing and pulling her hair at the roots. More aching bloomed throughout Casey, and she couldn't help but moan.

"He will watch us to get in the mood, then go off to tend to his own needs after. That is our opportunity."

Casey nodded, masking it as nuzzling his neck. So they would have to immediately abandon all post-orgasmic bliss the very moment that Black Rose got too horny to ignore his own desires.

"But how will we know when? He's watching from the next room over?"

John's hand settled on her crotch, covering her with ease. It was a simple gesture, but the proof of how broad his palm was, how thin and dexterous his fingers were, made her tremble in anticipation.

"That's easy. He always gets too excited to hold back after watching pretty women get their faces covered."

Casey was too much of a professional for her eyes to widen, but even a hardened expert like her could be surprised at her own eagerness. Being down on her knees with a man towering over her, watching his face pass the point of no return as his expression contorted, feeling the hot spurt of cum as it rained down. Closing your eyes at the last possible moment, bathing in the proof of your power over men... it was an indescribable feeling.

"Then let's not keep him waiting," she whispered, dragging her tongue down the side of his neck and making her way towards her goal. She wasn't going to rush things, but she was going to make sure that everyone knew exactly where this was headed.

With every inch that she drew closer to her goal, she grew more certain that John and Miranda were a little younger than they first appeared. It was subtle, but they used makeup and prosthetics to age themselves at least a decade. From a distance, it was effective enough, but nothing could conceal the truth when she was running her tongue over each and every rib, faintly tracing the bumps and dips that made up every man.

He squirmed beneath her, and over on the other bed, Miranda gasped as the loud, wet sucking of Ashton's ardor echoed loudly. He was having his way with her breasts, teasing and tempting her nipples to rise between his lips. Her peaks were his to conquer, and she would peak whether she liked it or not.

Casey didn't quite know when it had happened, but as she wrapped her lips around the head of another man's cock, she realized that she trusted these two. There was no other option, if they wanted to get out of here alive and finish their mission, she needed to put her complete faith in this British man, which included having him cum all over her face.

With that empowering surge, she set about giving the best damn blowjob that she'd ever given. She poured all the training that she'd gone through and all the natural intuition and experience that she'd accumulated over the years, she poured it all straight from her tongue into his thick, veiny cock.

It would have stretched her out down below, and that meant that her mouth was even less equipped to handle it. But Casey was nothing if not an expert at adapting to mission parameters that were less than ideal. If you couldn't shove the whole thing in your mouth, then you could still work absolute magic with a tongue and skillful kisses.

Peppering the length of his shaft, running up and down repeatedly, she alternated her approach. A kiss to the tip, a lavish lap of her tongue along the sensitive underside of his manhood, moaning all the while. She writhed on the bed, and somehow, she ended up almost parallel to him. Her head was at his crotch, but that also meant that her crotch was near enough for him to reach out and feel.

And that is precisely what he did. With those long fingers that had simply settled on her before, he delivered on his promise. He toyed with her at first, but he followed her pace, and it wasn't long before he was rubbing her clit between two fingers. He dipped inside her, forcing her entire body to arch with surprise and pleasure. In turn, she got her revenge with hot, heavy breaths that must have sent unimaginable chills down his spit-soaked cock. Sometimes, all you needed was a little air wafting across a wet surface.

"I can't... that's...."

John bucked beneath her, begging for release. Of course, because he was begging, she absolutely wasn't going to give it to him. Casey told herself that it was nothing more than the most effective method to complete the mission by ensuring that their observer was on the edge of his seat and waiting for the most powerful orgasm of all, but in truth, she enjoyed teased men so very much.

"You can," she crooned as she pulled away, a string of saliva running from her lips to the tip of his cock. Even separated, she could still manipulate him like a puppet at the end of a string.

Ashton had shown far less restraint, and even now, he had mounted Miranda and was pounding her down into the bed. Everything creaked as the woman beneath him moaned, timidly then with increasing abandon. Every twitch of his muscles was deliberate. Every driving thrust downward was measured to be exactly at the edge of what the poor woman could take.

Casey could see it in her mind's eye. This prim and proper British woman with a careful and well-endowed husband. He would make sure that she was good and ready each and every time, and there would never be a question of if she was wet and ready enough for lovemaking.

But it was not so with Ashton. As her fingernails tore holes in the blankets that she desperately clung to, as she gave up trying to protect her dignity by covering herself with what remained of her shirt. Everything about Miranda was put on display for the world to see. From experience, Casey knew that the woman must be wondering if she could possibly widen any more to accommodate such a driven and ruthless man. And again, Casey knew from experience that she could indeed fit the man in his entirety.

His pace quickened. Maybe it would have been imperceptible if she wasn't so familiar with the sexual quirks and irregularities of Ashton's rhythm, but she could see that he was closing in on the point of no return. Would he explosively fill Miranda, or would he pull out? Would he mark her face? Had she whispered to him the same details about what they must do?

And on top of that, Casey felt an urge to win, to be the first across the finish line. As if sensing that, John's fingers darted inside her once more, this time with crystal clear intent. He plunged in and out of her, over and over, brushing against her clit, and driving her straight to the edge. What else was there to do but put her head down and make herself useful?

A single moment was all it took for John to realize that she had merely been playing around before. When she truly applied herself, when she gave it her all, then there was no withstanding the vortex of suction and wet lust, of dancing fingers and lips that didn't give an inch.

The very moment that she took his cock into her mouth, he was undone. When John's entire body shook and twitched, so too did his fingers, and only then did Casey allow herself to give in to orgasm.

She watched from beneath half-closed lids as Miranda shattered, falling back to the bed and whimpering. Her eyes were open, and what little of her attention had not been stolen by Ashton was squarely on her husband. Not on the woman at his crotch, sucking the love right out of him, but on his face.

It was perverse, but Casey wanted to drag that attention down to her. The woman had done nothing wrong and was surely a victim here, but the agent still felt an urge to be the winner, to steal a man away by her skill alone.

And then he was spilling in her mouth, and she could think of nothing but the shocking volume he had to offer. It was suffocating and glazing, coating her throat and threatening to burst from her nostrils if she sneezed. It was altogether too much, but that only reinforced her sense of pride. He'd been saving up, and it had all gone to her.

She was the conqueror, she was the queen, and she would have what she was owed.

Chapter 16

It was a gut feeling, Ashton knew. Nothing more, nothing less. And yet, he was absolutely aware of just how great the difference was between him and Casey Anderson at that moment. She was a woman who gave herself completely to the mission, doing whatever it took to milk every last drop of cum if it meant that she could put a bullet between the eyes of their foe.

But for Ashton, a novice in almost every way to being on this side of the criminal equation, it felt like he was fucking a woman wearing a mask while watching the woman he loved suck another man dry. It was straight out of the most perverse nightmares that someone might have about the ultra-rich and their disgusting proclivities. Did Casey even see the masks anymore? Did she even care how twisted this all was?

He shoved the thoughts away, driving even harder into the mewling woman below him. Miranda was attractive by every objective measure, and everything about her should be arousing. The problem was that he was aroused. How could he get hard in such a situation, knowing that the woman didn't want to be doing this, that her own pain was exponentially greater than whatever jealousy he personally felt towards Casey and John?

It was with those thoughts that he forced himself to cum, closing his eyes and ears to the sounds of what was going on next to him. He forced himself hard and deep, but even so, the woman beneath him wriggled away. She freed herself, sliding down the mattress until he found himself on all fours with his crotch above her face.

She wanted him to give her a facial. He was too stunned to even react, too much of a gentleman to pin her down and empty inside her.

Perplexed, he allowed these events to play out. With his guard down, he couldn't help but look over and watch as Casey, dressed up for a ballroom dance, panted and gasped, her face glistening with what could only be another man's semen.

With a motion that could be nothing but practiced to the point where it appeared natural and absent-minded, she reached up and ran a finger down her cheek, gathering up thick whiteness as she went. Ashton could not look away as she drew it down to her lips. There was a glazed look in her eyes as she tasted it all as if she was high on the moment.

And then he looked down at the woman below him. Her eyes were shut tightly, and his cock was twitching and spasming out the last little bits of his own satisfaction. Had that sight of Casey pushed him over the edge?

What a remarkable sense of revulsion and arousal this stirred within him. It was almost enough to make him storm over to Casey and take her pussy for himself, to claim part of her for himself.

But that would not do. Slow, steadying breaths brought him back to the reality of the moment. It was difficult to hide everything beneath a veneer of orgasmic bliss, but if Miranda were correct, then right about now, Black Rose would be abandoning his observation and retiring to have his way with his own little playthings.

Ashton rolled over onto his back with a great sigh, laying roughly alongside Miranda.

"Is it time?" he whispered, covering it up by pulling her into a loose embrace.

As she rolled over to join him, he could feel his cum press against his skin, rapidly cooling in the air. "It is time. They should have two men posted outside, but they won't be particularly attentive. They're more there to make sure that no other guests accidentally stumble in here on their own carnal adventures than to prevent us from getting out."

Ashton closed his eyes and counted to ten. It was the last moment of peace that he would know for a long, long time. Once those seconds were past, there wouldn't be a single instant to spare.

The first order of business was Casey. He rolled from the bed and closed the distance in a single motion, bending down low and tugging her hair under the guise of jealous forcefulness. In truth, he just wanted to whisper into her ear, but his groping hands seizing her breasts and reclaiming her thighs made the charade quite convincing.

"You should go out the balcony, the same one that John and I used on the night we met. The slope below is gentle enough that you should be able to easily make your escape. Wait fifteen minutes. By then, John, Miranda, and I should have the thermal sensors down. Make a run for the prefabricated buildings and then take it from there. Don't worry about me. If you see an opportunity to break everyone out, then you should take your shot. Got it?"

From this close, it was quite disconcerting to have Casey watch him out of the corner of her eye. She almost looked like a predator watching her prey, and the lazy smile still gracing her lips did not help.

"Just make sure that you get it done, Adam," she said. Then before he could move, she gave him a quick peck on the lips. "I was wrong before. You're definitely ready for this line of work."

He wasn't exactly enthused to feel another man's cum on his cheek, but at least the cheekiness of the gesture did restore some of his normal confidence. This would be normal, and everything would be fine. He and Casey would get through this and get back to their old bantering ways. No sweat.

"They're not watching the cameras in this room anymore. We've jammed them," John said, holding a small remote.

As one, the four exploded into motion. Getting dressed, wiping faces down, checking to make sure that they all had their own private stashes of weapons only took a matter of moments. Before long, Ashton was repeating the beginning of the evening with Casey, the pair looking one another over for any mistakes.

It was incredible how quickly she had donned her dress once more. They had chosen black with the possibility in mind that she might need to hide outside. The moon would be full, so anything else would be too easy to spot from a distance.

"Don't hesitate if you have to pull the trigger," Casey said. "They may try some pretty dirty tricks."

"Worry about yourself. I've got backup," Ashton replied.

Together, they looked over at Miranda and John, who were quietly whispering to one another while she fixed his tie. Neither looked to be on the verge of tears but struck Ashton as profoundly empty as if they had gone through this so many times that they didn't even have it left in them to let their sorrow out.

"We'll get the bastard," Ashton hissed. One last reassuring pat of his hidden weapons, and then he made his way to the door. When he looked back, Casey was already gone. It would have been easy to make his way to the balcony and bid her farewell, but never had it been more critical to maintain a professional air and stick to the mission.

At the front door of the apartments, John and Miranda had already drawn tiny pistols and were ready on either side of the door.

"You know the shortest route to the security station, right?" Ashton asked, his fingers itching. At his wrist, a knife was ready to slide out at a moment's notice. He'd decided that the element of surprise would be most effective here. All he had to do was close the distance while appearing unarmed, and he could slit a man's throat before he even knew what hit him.

"That's right, just follow my lead," Miranda said. Her face was washed free of makeup now, and there was a grim determination to her gaze. "The guards outside have left to follow Black Rose."

Before Ashton could even ask what the plan was beyond that, John jerked the door open, and the couple stormed out into the hallway. There was nothing to do but follow.

What ensued felt more like a dream than reality. From the outside, they must have looked like disheveled guests, stumbling their way over rich carpets and barely managing not to knock over priceless vases.

And yet, they did not encounter anyone.

"We're taking a route that leads straight past the master's own rooms. They've shut down all security cameras here while he's attending to his personal pleasure," John said as they waited at a corner for another stumbling guest to clear out of the hallway before them.

One would think that they would want to maximize security at a time like that, Ashton thought.

Clearly, Miranda could read his thoughts. "None of his security can stand to even be within hearing distance of his room when he's having fun." If a face could look more disgusted than hers did at that moment, then Ashton had yet to see it.

He nodded, then peeked his head around the corner, only to find that a guard was advancing in their direction, hand resting comfortably on a holstered gun.

By sheer luck, Ashton managed to pull back before he was caught. A panicked survey of their immediate surroundings yielded nothing that promised total safety. They hadn't checked any of the doors, so they could very well be tumbling into a den full of armed thugs if they weren't careful.

There was nothing to do but follow the pair of Brits as they flattened themselves against the wall, making use of one of the slight alcoves used for showing off a piece of porcelain.

It was a tight fit, but the three of them were just out of sight if the guard was to pass by and not pay too much attention. However, if he stopped and took a close look, they were done for.

All three held their breath, all three listened intently to his padded footsteps, and all three exhaled at the same time when the sound began to grow quieter instead of louder.

"Close one," John whispered. "We'd better hurry."

Ashton couldn't disagree with that one bit. He followed as they took turn after turn, just catching the boots of guards that were passing through intersecting hallways. There were voices all around, but it was more the distant rumble of merrymaking than any parties close enough to actually stumble upon the three spies.

And then, they ran into a guard that was not moving. Instead, he stood in an intersection, trying his best to look casual as he leaned against an ornate pillar but clearly on the lookout for anything suspicious.

"Do let me handle this one, darlings," Miranda purred, then straightened herself out and instantly fell into a haughty stride with just a touch of drunken insouciance. "You there!"

The guard raised his eyebrows as he turned to watch the three approach. Ashton had reflexively followed John's lead, and a quick glance confirmed their strategy. With an apologetic grimace, the pair of men followed Miranda like attendants that wanted to stop their mistress from doing something foolish but lacked the authority to do so.

"You must forgive her," John said with a powerless gesture of surrender. "She really doesn't—

"Silence!" Miranda snapped, stomping her foot lightly. The carpet almost completely nullified the effect, and she was quite convincing in acting like that was the most grievous insult done to her in living memory.

The guard watched, his eyes narrowed, but he didn't look like he was about to draw and gun them down on the spot.

Miranda sauntered right up to him, then past him, making a show of looking his body up and down. She frowned, then leaned in closer for an inspection.

"Hm... Perhaps you would suffice for some fun this evening. Do you know how to handle your cock as well as that gun?"

It was quite impressive, Ashton decided after the fact. There was barely enough time to even process what was going on in the moment. For just a split second, he was shocked by the words coming out of the woman's mouth. After all, who wouldn't be? But a professional would be able to recover almost instantaneously.

Unfortunately, almost instantaneously simply wasn't good enough. By the time you got to almost instantaneously, the assuming man trying to apologize on her behalf could close the distance and shove an ice pick straight into the base of one's skull.

Ashton blinked, and then the guard was sagging against John, twitching as his muscles struggled to come to terms with the fact that his brain had just gone dark.

With brutal efficiency, John pushed the guard back up against the column, making him look like a drunk trying to brace himself. If the man crumpled into a pile on the ground, so be it. That would just enhance the illusion.

Whether the guard was already dead or breathing his last, it mattered not. The trio slipped deeper and deeper into the estate, winding their way around patrol after patrol.

Miranda halted and then motioned for them to back up and take a different path from time to time. It surely took no more than a handful of minutes to work their way to their destination, but it felt like a subjective eternity.

And then, they were peering down a corridor that terminated in a door that looked like any other, save for the pair of guards that were flanking it. By any measure, it simply looked like a room for some important guests or a meeting.

Then again, if Ashton were going to pick the location for a highly secure room from which to manage an entire complex's surveillance, his first step would be to find somewhere that didn't look particularly noteworthy.

"No way for us to sneak up on them this time," John whispered. "Can you handle them?"

Ashton frowned and took stock of the situation. It was a good fifteen yards to where the guards were posted, and there was nowhere to hide on the approach, no flanking angles whatsoever. It was too far for a man to rush and hope to escape unscathed.

"Yeah, I got this," he murmured, and then without any further ado, he lurched out into the open.

He didn't go for a full drunken stumbling, not this time. Instead, he just added a shuffling step or two, running a hand through his messy hair and pasting a leering grin on his face.

"Have you seen the women they've got here?" he slurred, looking from one guard to the other. "They fall all over you!"

The trick here was to keep his composure. Slowly putting one foot in front of the other was excruciating. At any moment, one of the guards might just raise his gun and take a shot. Nothing was keeping him safe but the illusion that he was a harmless guest eager to brag about his sexual conquests. If there was one thing that he knew exactly how to do, it was to appear pathetic given the tools at hand.

"They literally just give them to you if you pay enough," he chuckled, pausing to brace himself against a wall, slowing his progress even further but banking on it reducing his apparent threat level even further. "Can you believe that? As long as you've got the money, you can get all the pussy you want!"

"Yeah, that's how it works, dipshit," one of the guards muttered under his breath. "Kinda the whole fucking point."

Ashton frowned as if struggling to hear and understand. Then, he grinned broadly once more, spreading his arms and lurching forward. He was halfway there but not nearly close enough to actually execute his plan.

To their credit, the guards did fidget. They weren't hiding that they had guns, but they weren't shoving them in his direction quite yet. It must have been a tricky situation for them. They definitely would pay if they offed an important guest who was just stumbling at them, but at the same time, they had to protect what was inside.

"Hey, if you guys could point me in the direction of—"

"Fuck off, buddy," the second guard hissed, then slammed a fist into the door at his side.

It was a signal to someone inside, probably that they needed to send someone out to deal with the riff-raff and drag him away before he could cause too much of a commotion. Unfortunately for the guard, it was also precisely the opportunity Ashton had been waiting for.

He hurled himself forward, convincing enough as a drunk who had lost his balance, but his real goal was to keep his center of gravity low and present a smaller target. The poor bastard that had banged on the door was struggling to get his hand back on his holster and draw his weapon. That meant that he was less dangerous and would have to bear witness to what his mistake had cost his partner.

Ashton drove his fist into the other guard's arm as he raised his pistol. It would have been quite inconvenient for a shot to go off and alert everyone else, so Ashton intentionally drove his hidden knife through the man's wrist, severing his tendons and rendering his trigger finger useless.

He opened his mouth to scream in shock and pain, maybe even with the intent of selflessly warning his comrades, but Ashton had another hand for that. Cover the mouth, slit the throat, just like in the old days.

It was almost enough to make him feel bad for the surviving guard. In his wide eyes, he could see fear and a glimmer of understanding. Fingers shook as he tried to steady his gun, but the distance was too short.

Ashton felt no sense of remorse as he severed the man's windpipe and dropped him to the ground. There had been plenty of time to shout a warning, but the absolute horror of the moment would have been enough to completely cloud the man's faculties.

Pure instinct snapped his attention back over his shoulder, where Miranda was standing with arm outstretched, gun pointing straight at him, her face utterly devoid of emotion. Cold, clinical professionalism permeated her posture, and her hand didn't tremble even a bit.

Crack.

The sound was barely audible, and Ashton was left dumbly wondering how that could be possible. As he died, was he going to be thinking about something as inane as why the gun that killed him didn't make more noise?

And then he realized it. There was a thud on the other side of the door, and he understood that the gun hadn't been pointed straight at him. Rather, she had shot right past him, taking out a guard standing on the other side of the security door, about to get the drop on him.

"Thanks," he said breathlessly.

"Don't mention it," Miranda replied, striding purposefully towards the door, John in her wake. While the wife inspected the bullet hole and tinkered with the handle, her husband began to lift one of the guards.

Right, they would probably need to drag them into the room to buy themselves a few moments of extra time. If a patrol came by and saw that there was nobody standing guard, they might be able to sow a bit of confusion among the subordinates of Black Rose. However, if they immediately saw that they were under attack, they would be bearing the full brunt of the organization's focused attention.

Before Ashton could even lift his own man, the door opened, and Miranda slipped inside. Two more soft cracks echoed, and then her voice carried softly. "Clear."

The room itself was about what he had expected. An entire wall was dominated by screens, showing dozens upon dozens of angles of the estate complex. It wasn't nearly enough to cover everything, but he noted that they were cycling through various cameras as well.

In his cursory glance, he was relieved to see that none were able to spot Casey as she waited on the balcony. Shit, it hadn't been fifteen whole minutes yet, had it?

"We're on a timer now. It will only be a matter of time until they figure out what's going on here and converge on our location," John said, taking a seat in front of a computer terminal.

"How long will it take to clear the sensors in Casey's path?" Ashton asked, no longer even bothering to use her code name. If he couldn't trust these two, he couldn't trust anyone.

John bent down to the body he had dragged in, then inspected his hands. With a shrug, he lifted one, slapped it down on the part of the computer, and was rewarded with an affirmative beep.

"We're in now, so it should only take a moment."

Miranda had taken another chair and was tapping away at a keyboard, leaving Ashton the odd man out.

"And... we're good," John said. "Thermal sensors are off, and it's too dark out for the optical cameras to pick up on Casey if she knows what she's doing. It's all up to her now."

Ashton felt a sudden chill run down his spine. "And now what do we do?"

"We," Miranda began with a grim smile, "have to buy her time."

"Shit," Ashton muttered. On the screens, the partying guests were slowly beginning to ask questions as armed men hurried past them. Based on what he understood of the estate's layout, they were definitely headed this way.

Chapter 17

Casey huddled in the corner of the balcony, crouched down and keeping a mental count in her head. Fourteen minutes had passed, and there was no indicator that anything had changed on the inside. When the moment came, she would throw herself over the edge, duck into a roll, and make a mad dash for cover. If the sensors were off, then she would live. If not, then she would die. It was as simple as that.

Could she trust them with this much? Should she try to find an alternate solution?

With a deep, steadying breath, she found her answer. Regardless of how much she trusted these two British agents, she still trusted Ashton to figure something out. They were a team, and she had to believe in his abilities.

Her mental clock struck fifteen, and then there was nothing left to do but let her honed reflexes take over.

With a swish of her dress, she was over the balcony edge and plunging down a handful of feet to hit the soft, freshly-cut grass that made up the lawn. The incline was less severe than she had been expecting, so she was able to control her fall and end in a semi-graceful roll.

Then, she was on her feet and off like an arrow. Her lungs burned and ached, and she was reminded of how taxing it was to orally pleasure a man and breathe simultaneously.

And yet, this was what she trained for. With every pump of her long legs, she felt all her fleeting worries fade away. Pain and exertion, the idea of physically progressing towards the completion of her mission, was what gave her the satisfaction and willpower to carry on.

The treeline approached, and with it, safety from prying eyes. However, no sooner did she reach the overhanging branches than she spied the flimsy metal and plastic that made up her goal. It had been lurking just out of sight since she'd arrived, but now she was finally within touching distance of the people she had been sent to save.

Crouching down, she advanced closer and ensured that there were no wary guards nearby. As best she could tell, there were a dozen roughly identical structures, all more or less long rectangles arranged in rows like a barracks. Presently, she was at the end of the main avenue leading between them, with all the buildings branching off like little streets. It was an organized little system, and the heavy tree cover all around likely covered it from view by planes and satellites above.

Patrols came, and patrols went. These men were holding heavy rifles at all times, not caring to hide their violent potential like those inside the estate tending to the party guests. Their goal was to shoot down any slaves that tried to escape, that much was clear.

Once Casey was quite sure that she had their pattern down, she made her move. The dirt paths were lit but not particularly thoroughly. They likely didn't want to use too much illumination in case it drew attention to this theoretically secret warehouse of human flesh.

Darting from the cover of the trees to the cold of metal, Casey kept low and followed one guard as he made his meandering way around the back of one of the buildings. Based on what she'd observed so far, he would keep going, and she would have about thirty seconds to find a way into the adjacent building before the next guard in the patrol came up behind her.

But as was often the case with plans conjured on the fly, just a few moments of observation were not enough to get a perfect idea of what her enemies were doing.

Rounding that corner and expecting to find the backside of a guard sauntering along on his merry way, Casey instead came face-to-face with the man. He must have just turned around and been ready to re-trace his steps. Whether it was because he'd forgotten something or because the patrol routes mixed things up by design, it did not matter.

All that mattered was Casey's palm rising like a bolt of lightning, striking the guard under the chin. The whites of his eyes shone bright in the moonlight, and the sickening snap of his neck snapping backward was surpassed only by the brutal crack of his skull striking the ground.

Breathing heavily, Casey waited for her brain to catch up with her muscles. He was dead and was going to be incredibly difficult to cover up. Thinking quickly, she turned to the building, where there was thankfully an ajar.

However, Casey was much less thankful to see a pair of eyes watching her from the darkness inside. With one fluid motion, she reached down and drew the tiny pistol that she kept strapped to her thigh.

It was sheer luck and gut instinct that kept her from immediately raising it and firing. Instead, she peered into the darkness and realized that something was off.

Unless she was very much mistaken, then the pair of eyes looking back at her were far too low to be an adult. It had to be a child, which meant that she had nearly blown away one of the human trafficking victims.

"Help me drag this body in there," she whispered, not bothering to waste any time seeing if she was obeyed.

With only thirty seconds, she didn't have a single moment to spare before the next guard came. Gripping the shoulders of the dead bastard, she yanked him towards the door.

One pair of hands joined her, then another. She was only vaguely aware of the emaciated figures that lent their aid. There would be time enough for taking stock of the situation once they were inside.

Just as the stamping of patrolling feet outside drew close enough to make out, they yanked the dead guard inside and shut the door. Then, all was bathed in darkness.

"Who are you?" a heavily accented voice whispered, so close that she could feel it puffing on her skin.

"Did you come to save us?" another whispered, this one young and coming from so low that it had to be a child.

This changed things. If the victims were immediately ready to leap into action and help her hide a body, then they might also be prepared to break out of here this very evening. If that was the case, then there was no sense in waiting.

It killed her to leave Ashton behind, but she had to have trust in him, just like he had trusted her.

Biting her tongue, she squinted and felt her eyes adjusting to the darkness. There were dozens in the room with her, most holding themselves at a distance.

"Yes, I'm here to break you all out of here, but if you want to succeed, you'll have to do exactly what I say."

Chapter 18

"There's no way we can possibly hold them here," Ashton snarled, blindly emptying a stolen handgun down the hallway.

John stood across from him, responsible for the opposite approach. At the little T-intersection they had chosen to make their stand, they could not let a single enemy through, or else they would have a straight shot at Miranda, who was still ensconced in the security room and doing her damnedest to distract and disrupt Black Rose security forces. Based on the sheer number of goons that were bearing down on them at this moment, it seemed that she was doing a pretty good job. If this much manpower was being dedicated to taking down this trio, then they must not have figured out what Casey was up to.

Either that or they'd already caught her. Ashton pushed the thought away before it could undermine his confidence.

John peeked out, delivered two more fatal shots to guards that had drawn a little too close, then pulled back into cover. The answering barrage of shots sent wallpaper splintering and smashed ceramic into nothingness, but neither of them had been hit quite yet.

They'd killed more than a dozen, but those had been only the most foolish of their enemies. The smarter ones were taking cover and waiting for the heavy weapons to come. Once they decided to use grenades or gas, then this was all over.

"Come here!" Miranda cried. "I found something!"

With a shared glance, John and Ashton retreated to the security room. They might have a few moments before the guards realized they were shooting at nothing, but hopefully, it would be enough.

"What is it?" Ashton asked, but the words had barely left his mouth before he realized what he was looking at.

Miranda and John were both crouched down, examining a tiny passage that led out of the room.

"I think this leads straight to the exterior. It's an escape route for Black Rose himself," Miranda mused. "I'd heard about these, but I had no idea where they actually were."

There was no time to hesitate. "I'll go first in case there's any danger," Ashton said, already getting down on his hands and knees before the tiny opening. God damn, did he hate confined spaces.

"Alright, but hurry," Miranda said, giving him a reassuring pat on the shoulder. "We'll be right behind you."

Chapter 19

Casey looked all around her. It was almost surreal. The level of carnage had surpassed anything that she was expecting. All her fears about the slaves not being willing to rise up and come to her aid had been so woefully misplaced that it was almost comical.

Before she had even finished explaining her plan, the men and women had poured out of the entrance and screamed. At first, she'd thought it was just reckless glee, but then cries rose up through the rest of the compound. As one, hundreds of the oppressed threw off their shackles and broke through doors and locks that they had spent every waking moment sabotaging and filing down.

Blood drenched the dirt, glistening in the moonlight, but very little of it belonged to the slaves. Just like she had surprised her victim, so too did the slaves drown their captors in a human tide before anything more than a few shots could be fired.

And now, she stood with her mission accomplished, leading hundreds of starving, bloody, tortured souls as far from the estate as she could.

She'd stolen a radio from one of the guards, and every few moments, she checked in on the encrypted frequency that Carlisle had given her. Every few moments, she was met with failure, and they ran over ragged hill after hill. The trees didn't seem to be growing any less dense, and the moon seemed to glow brighter and brighter.

"Agent Anderson? Agent Anderson, come in!"

It took her a moment for her fatigued brain to process that it was coming from the radio. Unable to focus on more than one thing at once, she dropped to her knees and fiddled with settings, trying to make the signal louder.

"Yes, sending verification now," she said, her voice hoarse and scratchy. Was the moon even still up, or was it morning? How long had they been running for?

She looked around while she waited for her handlers to get back to her, and in the daylight, she saw the most macabre assortment of human beings that she'd ever beheld in her life. Of every race and every creed, of every age and appearance, the only thing they had in common was how horrifically they had been treated and how the light was slowly glowing in their eyes once more.

But they weren't all here, were they? Servants like Veronica, the ones who had been in the estate during the jailbreak, none of them were here.

"Identity confirmed. Welcome back, Casey." This time, it was Carlisle's voice, and she could practically see his exhausted face as he sagged back in his office chair and finally gave up his long vigil. The sentimental fool always lost too many hours of sleep over his agents.

Over the next several minutes, they negotiated the extraction of the trafficking victims with her. They would all be picked up in a convoy of buses that had been repurposed for this mission. At the same time, law enforcement waiting on standby would converge on the estate and deal with the remnants of the Black Rose organization, advancing slowly to not let a single member escape.

Casey closed her eyes, trying to take solace in the fact that she had won. But she had left her partner behind. Ashton was still there, maybe dead, maybe being tortured, maybe still running and hiding and fighting, waiting for her to save the day. It may be too late by the time the cavalry actually showed up.

"Something wrong?" Carlisle asked. The man always could sense when things were amiss.

"Just one thing," Casey said. "I want you to look up two agents with British intelligence...."

Chapter 20

Ashton blinked, immediately regretting his choice. The light was blinding, and his head was throbbing. Where the hell was he? The last thing he could remember...

Ah, right. He probably should have seen that one coming.

"You're a tough nut to crack, Mister Malick," a familiar voice chuckled from the darkness before him. The light was there to blind Ashton, not to let him actually see anything around him.

"We meet again, Black Rose. I hope you enjoyed your little show, considering how much it ended up costing you," Ashton said weakly. He was desperate for a drink of water. How much time had passed since he'd originally parted from Casey? How long had he been out?

Heavy breathing was the only sound from the other side of the room. It gave him a moment to take in his circumstances, if nothing else. Tied up to a chair, naturally. There was a table before him, the rickety metal sort that one might find in any interrogation chamber the world over.

"I've had better," Miranda said from somewhere off to the right if that was her real name. She'd been the one to hit him on the back of his head if his foggy memory served.

He'd been expecting some sort of betrayal. After all, it was part of the job, but that didn't make it hurt any less.

"Did you really need to shut down all the communications?" Black Rose muttered. "Can't get a damn message from the slave compound."

"Then specify that beforehand," Miranda snapped. "You just said to make it look real."

Ashton suppressed the urge to snort and make some snarky comment about how they weren't particularly good at this interrogation business.

And hell, what did they even want from him? It wasn't like he had any useful details to give them. Then again, this may just be a matter of torture for personal enjoyment. The urge to cringe at that was simply too strong to be subdued.

The door opened with an ominous creak, somewhere off to his left. Perhaps that's where John was.

Whispered voices carried, but not well enough for Ashton to make out what they were saying.

"Shit," John hissed under his breath. Yep, he was by the door.

"What is it?" Black Rose and Miranda asked as one. Though it scarcely mattered, Ashton found himself wondering if the pair of Brits were even actually married. Then again, maybe that was just the potential brain damage talking.

More footsteps, then more whispering, the more cursing. And then, the door slammed, and all was silent.

Was he alone in the room? Had they all left, or did they just want him to think they had?

More footsteps echoed, but this time they were shuffling and tentative. More importantly, they were behind him.

"Are you alright?" a voice whispered, so soft and sweet that he could have cried.

"I'm fine, Veronica," he said hoarsely. It didn't even matter if she was in on everything as well. He couldn't believe that she might have betrayed him as well and been part of this conspiracy from the very start. If she was, he might as well just die on the spot anyway.

"Here, let me help you," she whispered, and then her fingers were against his wrist and trembling. The bindings were tight, cutting off his circulation, but she was ferocious and ripped at them with her fingernails.

"Won't they see you doing this? Surely they have surveillance in here."

"No, it seems that nothing is working. Everyone is quite panicked about it. That's what Black Rose and his henchmen went to investigate."

Ashton nodded. What else could he do? Maybe he was about to be lured into another trap, but at least his hands would be free. And this time, he would be cautious about getting into any small openings where he couldn't move his arms or protect himself.

"Why are you here?" he couldn't help but ask.

Her lips moved even closer to his ear, and her words came even softer than before. Nobody could have heard them unless they were inches away.

"Because your partner sent me."

Ashton blinked. Casey had given orders to Veronica? When could she have possibly...

"How long was I out? Did she get caught too? What the hell—"

Before a single one of his questions could be answered, the door slammed open once more. Veronica retreated with a muffled gasp, and then Ashton could barely make out the looming silhouette of none other than Black Rose storming into the room.

"Christ, do you wear that mask all the time?" Ashton muttered. His hands weren't quite free, but they were close. If he was lucky, then he might be able to break free. All he had to do was bide his time until that point.

Why Veronica helped him didn't matter. Maybe she was a traitor, maybe not. Maybe she just wanted him to kill the bastard so there could be a change in leadership. Perhaps she was just a scared girl that wanted to help someone who had helped her.

That last thought sobered Ashton up. As far as he could tell, she was still behind him, waiting patiently like the servant she was. Or at least trying to.

If he managed to break free and kill someone, he would eventually be caught, and Veronica would probably be executed or worse.

"Where is she?" Black Rose snarled, leaning across the table. His eyes gleamed with madness, and he clenched his fists repeatedly.

"Let me guess. You finally got in contact with your little slave compound and found out that Casey managed to break them all out?"

Black Rose slammed a fist down on the table. In his peripheral vision, Ashton could see Miranda and John moving around the sides of the room. They had him surrounded, there was no way that he could kill all three before being taken down. But maybe all that really mattered was getting rid of the villain before him.

At the very least, it would be slightly less humiliating to die this way than to go out having completely failed at his mission.

Ashton tensed, waiting for Black Rose to draw just a little bit closer. Just a tiny bit more, and then he would have him. Crushing his throat would likely do the trick, especially since they must have taken his knife away. Ah well, there really was nothing for it.

He insolently looked over at John, just to infuriate his primary target by ignoring him. "Between the two of us, I think I got the better end of the deal in that bedroom. Casey's tits can't hold a candle to your wife's."

John twitched, but only slightly. Interesting, maybe they did have a thing going on.

And then, an earthshaking boom rocked Ashton's entire world.

His bones vibrated with noise, and without an instant of delay, he ripped himself out of his restraints, leaping forward and wrapping his hands around Black Rose's neck. Fury dissipated in those eyes, replaced by absolute fear. Then pure emptiness.

Gunshots rang out, but Ashton felt a peculiar sense of ease. If this was how he was going to die, then so be it. All he could hope to do was inflict as much damage as possible on the man before him.

But he really shouldn't still be standing, should he? And shouldn't there be a bit more shouting and chaos?

Ashton glanced over and saw John sliding down to the floor, a red hole in the center of his forehead. Likewise, on his other side, Miranda had collapsed into a twitching heap, blood, and foam gurgling from her mouth.

Now that he was on his feet, he could swat that pesky light out of his face up above. With it gone, he suffered from a moment of blindness, but then he could truly take in the scene around him.

Was it Veronica? No, she was cowering behind him, in a corner. At least she had some good instincts there.

"Ashton?" a voice called out. And really, what other voice could it have been?"

"Casey?"

When she stepped out of the doorway, stained with blood and dirt, pistol in one hand and eyes searching for threats, she looked like a warrior goddess coming straight from his imagination. It was all too much. Much too much.

Ashton sank back down into the chair that had just been his prison with a sigh. Behind him, Veronica scrambled to her feet and hurried to one side while Casey appeared on the other.

"What did I do to earn two women spoiling me?" he gasped, suddenly feeling all his pain catching up to him.

"Is he going to be alright?" Veronica asked, but it sounded like her voice was underwater. Slowly, everything was fading away.

"Unfortunately, yes," Casey snorted. "He's just tired." And then, suddenly, her voice was much closer, coming straight into his ear. "But you did a good job, Agent Malick. We got 'em."

With a smile on his lips, Ashton felt all his exhaustion catching up to him. He really needed a vacation after this. Maybe even one with Casey again.

Excerpt from
Seducing Vegas

Chapter 1

Harrison Siegel was living the life. Hot women, fast cars, high-stakes gambling, and the best alcohol that money could buy, what more could a guy want?

Absolutely nothing, Harrison decided emphatically as he poured himself another shot and looked down from the hotel balcony onto the pulsing, beating heart of the city. It was his favorite time of night when the scorching Nevada heat finally died down for a few precious hours. One day, it would all be his. One day, he would be looking down from the penthouse of the Chateau, his family's casino.

Not for the first time, he rolled the glass in his hand and gave serious thought to his future. Fears and insecurities, the dread of drowning when thrust in over his head, and a detached sense of frustration with a father that expected but never understood... but then he crushed those thoughts and took another drink. He didn't drink to wash away darker thoughts. He didn't sleep with a newer and more beautiful woman every night to make himself forget. Those were the actions of a weak man, and he was anything but weak.

The problem with indulging in the best whiskey around, he mused to himself as he turned away and stumbled his way back into the hotel room, was that one tended to build up a bit of a tolerance. It took more and more to get to sleep each time.

No, it took more and more to get drunk, he corrected as he lumbered over to the bed, where a pair of pairs rose and fell in light sleep.

It had been a good night so far. What was the red-head's name? Rose? Probably not her real name, but she'd looked so good up on that stage that he'd just had to find out if she was half as provocative in bed. To everyone's mutual pleasure, she had been.

The blonde, though, she had been a bit of a let-down. All that sensual flirting down on the dance floor had quickly fallen apart in the bedroom, where she'd been as shy as could be. Oh well, there was still a little fun to be had in showing an inexperienced girl just how good things could really be. Plus, Harrison took a small measure of perverse pleasure in the notion that he might have just ruined this girl for relationships going forward. Every time she was with a man, she'd look back on this and sigh wistfully.

Harrison knew he wasn't a good person. He knew it in his bones, because after all, what could the alternative possibly be? His father wasn't a good person, the world around him didn't make good people, and good people never got what they wanted in life. The real question lately had been a matter of figuring out just what kind of bad he wanted to be.

But there was enough time for such rumination later. For now, he had a third-round to enjoy. Or was it the fourth?

Setting his empty glass aside, Harrison returned to the warmth of his bed and coaxed two piles of sleeping limbs into a single writhing melding of passion, feminine scent, dark tattoos, and temporary pleasure.

An hour later, Harrison took a leisurely elevator ride down to the lobby. He couldn't even remember what hotel he'd stumbled into around midnight. It certainly hadn't been the Chateau, but that was all he knew for certain.

"Mary," he muttered under his breath. He had eventually coaxed the name from the blonde, but it was very much a matter of politeness and maintaining the illusion. Now she'd think that he wanted to remember her name for some future liaison or, even worse, so that he could daydream about her. Well, it cost him nothing to give her that little measure of hopeful happiness, but he would certainly never be seeing her again.

Rose though... that was another story altogether. Ah well, he knew precisely which stage to find her on if he ever got in the mood for a repeat performance. There was no need to think too much about it quite yet, and no, what he needed to think about right now was coffee.

At the chime, he stumbled out into the plush and garish lobby. He still had no idea where he was, but he knew all the layouts by instinct. Barely swaying at all, he made his way to the 24-hour cafe, where he knew that two things of critical importance were waiting for him: caffeine and solitude.

You see, everyone in Vegas knew who he was. At least, everyone who was anyone knew what he was, and that included the employees of all the hotels. When they saw a tattooed, shaved-headed, bleary-eyed hulk of a man walk through their doors at closer to dawn than midnight, everyone knew that it was none other than the wayward heir to good ole Bugsy.

Thank god for the soft, inoffensive lighting, Harrison thought to himself as he stepped into the high class and most unoccupied lounge. There was nothing more than the usual collection of late-night denizens scattered around, ranging from meek little night owls to the depressed and those in need of a quick sobering.

The barista was cute, a sultry redhead that leaned heavily on the counter, giving him the faintest shadow of a glance down the front of her perfectly proper blouse. If she'd been bursting with energy and leaping to take his order, then he might have turned around and walked away on the spot, but Vegas hotels knew their business. They knew what sort of clientele they had and what they wanted.

"Black, large," he said gruffly, not particularly surprised at how rough his voice sounded. It had been a long, wonderful night.

The redhead's lips curled slowly, doing terrible, terrible things to his insides. How very cruel of her to tease him when the simple act of blood flowing was enough to make him ache. Then again, the idea that she might be doing that on purpose...

Yes, she would certainly be making the list in the near future. She seemed like a woman that had a thing or two to teach him, and the opposite was a foregone conclusion. If he could just get her number—

A terrifyingly warm laugh echoed from behind, instantly raising every hair on the back of his neck. He would recognize that laugh anywhere, and the last thing in the world he wanted was to meet its owner. After all, he may not have been a good person, but he wasn't utterly heartless.

Not waiting for his drink, Harrison strode away without a purpose in mind. He just had to find somewhere to hide, that's all.

Shit, the bathrooms were the other way. There was nothing in this section but a smattering of booths and tables, less than a quarter occupied, and none by more than one or two people.

He'd just have to sit down at one and blend in. Natasha probably wasn't going to wander in here after him, but if she did...

Damn, he really had toyed with her, hadn't he? It would have been easy to tell that bright-eyed woman that he really wasn't looking for the same sort of commitment that she was. Hell, he'd been in the right about that too, a single week of passion was no reason to assume you were a permanent item. But, as was his way, he'd picked the even easier path and lied that he was leaving town and never coming back. Foolish of him to assume that she'd go back to wherever his home was — and that he'd already forgotten was surely a testament to how not good he was — but there you have it: Harrison Siegel could be quite the foolish man if pressed.

Which table to take though? Probably not one with a dangerous bastard like himself. The last thing he needed was to get into a fistfight, and not just because that would surely draw Natasha's attention, with those soft green eyes...

Shit, he was even starting to remember bits and pieces about her. That was never permissible.

His eye snagged on a timid little creature of a woman, not quite huddled up in the corner of a booth, but damn close. She watched everything with wide-eyed wonder, and he instantly knew her type. Harrison did not like tourists, and that went now more than ever. She had definitely watched his arrival, and if Natasha wandered in, she'd likely notice the same thing and ask this girl if a furtive bastard of a man with too many tattoos and reeking of booze and sweat had fled through here. And so, with his drunken haze not quite completely dispelled by fear and adrenaline, Harrison sat down across from her in the booth, ensuring that his back was to the rest of the room and that shadows covered the most obvious of his features.

"New in town?" he asked with a cheery suaveness that was painfully difficult to fake for a man like him, especially in a state such as his.

Her eyes widened, and her shocked silence gave him plenty of time to admire everything past her immediate usefulness to his schemes. The contrast between her hair and skin was nothing short of startling, with violently red waves cascading down one shoulder while her skin was pale enough that she couldn't have stepped outside in the past month. Her lips drew him, but that was nothing new. He always did enjoy imagining just what a woman was capable of right off the bat. Fewer disappointments that way.

She was definitely a tourist, that much was abundantly clear. The way she looked at him was borderline offensive, for he was absolutely certain that she was viewing him as an exciting look into the denizens of a dangerous den of vice and sin. If she had any common sense, she'd be looking for an escape route or perhaps a way to signal the barista for help.

But no, she was just staring at him with those big, beautiful...

Harrison sighed. Having a healthy sex drive could be quite the pain in the ass sometimes, but it was much more a pain in the dick at times like these.

Chapter 2

"New here?" he prompted again.

To her credit, she didn't jump out of her seat in surprise and embarrassment, which had happened a couple of times with the touristy types. Instead, she just nodded numbly. Harrison sensed that it was mostly sheer chance that her jaw wasn't on the floor.

"Are you an actor?"

Whatever he had been expecting her to say, that was most definitely not it.

"Beg your pardon?"

"An actor, you know, like the...." Her voice dropped as she leaned across the table, very nearly conspiratorially. "The shows. The performances? Is this one of them right now? Is it like a spontaneous little show?"

Harrison was mental inches away from raising an exasperated hand to an even more exasperated face, but then he caught himself.

"Yeah, something like that," he said with a wry grin. "I'm surprised you caught on so quick. You've got a good eye, you know that? Very perceptive."

She blushed, just as he knew she would. It was unfortunate that she was so easy to pin down. She really was quite lucky that she'd run into him before anyone else that might take real advantage of her naivete. Hell, was this her first day in town or something?

"Cause that's what we're all about in Vegas, spontaneous entertainment out of the goodness of our hearts," he said quickly, adding some much-needed bitterness to prevent his heart from showing too much.

"Oh no, I thought you'd politely but firmly ask for donations afterward," she said without blinking.

Harrison was momentarily taken aback, but only momentarily. He couldn't help but chuckle. "Well, maybe I pegged you wrong then. Sounds like you're not quite as defenseless as you might have first seemed."

"Certainly not!" With that, she lowered her voice and looked around before whispering. "Am I doing alright? I'm not exactly sure what kind of role I'm supposed to be playing here. If I'm being honest, I haven't exactly done this sort of thing before."

"One would never guess," Harrison said dryly. He dared a glance behind him, but there was no sign of Natasha. Maybe she'd left, and this was all just a big coincidence. Or perhaps she was hunting him down in every hotel she could find. Terrifying.

"So, what exactly do you need me to do?"

He turned his attention back to the girl. Actually, on second thought, was she a girl? He'd pegged her as unduly young and wet behind the ears, but she had to be over twenty, right? She certainly didn't look like she was fresh out of high school.

"Well, it's actually not all that complicated. You see, this isn't a big performance, and really, it's just for you."

"Me?" She breathed the word so softly that Harrison nearly closed his eyes just to focus on it.

"Yes, you. You see, it's a bit of a... well, I'm not sure how else to put it, but I'm supposed to give you an experience. You know, to pay attention to you and such. Just for a few minutes," he added hastily, lest he give yet another woman the wrong idea.

"But why?"

Harrison eyed her but couldn't quite make heads or tails of her reaction. She sounded neither disappointed nor excited. If anything, she sounded... curious? Though he wracked his mind, he couldn't remember a single time that a woman had treated him with simple curiosity, especially not when he was sitting alone with her in a booth with lighting that could easily be described as romantic, and especially not when he'd just made such a bald-faced overture.

"Why what?"

"I mean, what's the angle? This seems overly intimate for a crowd-pleasing performance, and how are you supposed to get a bunch of donations if I'm the only one who really experiences it? The whole thing doesn't seem like an efficient scheme."

"It's..." he mentally backpedaled, in more ways than one. Somehow, he didn't think that the last vestiges of his whiskey binge was to blame for this disorientation.

"It's to make you feel more at ease so that you go to a casino later and spend lots of money."

"But this hotel doesn't have a casino."

"It has a partnership with the one next door," he lied without hesitation. "The idea is the same as the cheap prime rib dinners, it's all to funnel you over there. And besides, the theory is that you wouldn't keep this to yourself, right? You'd tell other people that this wonderful experience happened to you, and then you'd go home and tell the same thing to people there, and they'd book trips to Vegas immediately."

It frightened him how easily it was to come up with such manipulation, both in terms of what he was doing to this girl and the feasibility of such a plan for running a casino. He was thinking more and more like his father, and that could not be permitted.

Still, she seemed a little dubious at his explanation, which eased his mind somewhat. Maybe she wouldn't get chewed up and spit out by the City of Sin. Maybe she would get back on her flight to whatever small town she hailed from. All she would have to remember her little adventure would be a mysterious conversation with an enigmatic tattooed man in a hotel cafe at three in the morning.

Closer to four, he corrected as he checked his phone.

And then he heard her voice. It would seem that he hadn't been lucky enough for this all to be a co-incidence.

"So, darling, tell me how your vacation to Vegas has been so far." He leaned forward, focusing the breadth of his considerable attention upon her. It was a technique that had never failed him to date, and this was looking to be no exception.

Her eyes widened, and for an instant, he almost felt ashamed that he was doing this without even asking the girl's name. On second thought, that was ridiculous. He'd done far more with women that he'd exchanged far fewer words with.

"It's been..." she trailed off as she glanced over his shoulder and frowned. Damn, she was definitely watching the approach of Natasha.

"She's part of the performance," Harrison reassured her, immediately drawing her gaze back to him. Perfect.

"Oh." The girl frowned, which was all too becoming on those lips. "But she looks so angry."

Harrison suppressed a sigh. "Yes, well, she's very good at her job. Now, tell me where you've visited so far. Had any wild nights of debauchery yet? Lost or won any fortunes at roulette? Or are you more of a poker kind of gal?"

Her eyes widened further with every word, and by the end of his questioning, her lips were parted. How on earth was he still able to get harder? A mystery to be solved another day, that.

"N-no, my flight just got in this evening. I went up to my room to sleep, but I guess I was too excited, or my body hadn't adjusted to the hours, so I came down here to people watch."

"Just a word to the wise, you might not want to tell strangers exactly where you're staying. Especially strange men."

She frowned at that. He really should get around to asking her name at some point. "But I'm here, sitting in the hotel's cafe. Doesn't that obviously mean I'm staying here?"

"Hardly. Plenty of people come to visit hotels for... one reason or another." No need to explain that he knew that from firsthand experience, especially not that his latest experience in that department wasn't even half an hour old. Hell, she could probably smell it on him if she put her mind to it.

"For... that?" From the expression on her face, she understood him well enough.

Perversely, Harrison felt a compulsion to sit around and chat with her about nothing at all. It was rare to run into a girl that didn't treat him with a combination of longing and fear. Hell, it was rare for him to run into anyone that didn't see him first and foremost as a walking bad reputation.

What did this girl see him as, anyway? Did she think everything about him was a ruse? That he was just an actor playing a part? Ha, she probably even thought his tattoos were props for the job, temporaries that would wash off later. Wouldn't that be something?

"She's coming over here," she whispered quickly, dragging him out from his uncharacteristic daydreams. "What should I say?"

"You—" Harrison caught himself. His original plan of lying low and blending in was now thoroughly shot. There was no way that this girl would be able to keep a straight face and play dumb at this point. One look at her, and Natasha would know that she'd found who she was looking for. Time for Plan B, then.

He took a deep breath and looked her square in the eye. What would have been trivially easy last night, or even a few hours ago, now felt oddly immoral. Probably due to the exact nature of his dispute with Natasha, but it wasn't like the girl in front of him was a nutjob that would lose it when she found out this wasn't real. Probably.

"You should act interested in me, and I will act interested in you. Very interested."

She blushed, but then her brow furrowed, and she looked at him with deep concern. "Er, this is all an act, right? She's not your girlfriend, and you're toying with her, right?"

Shit, she was a little more intuitive than he'd thought. Well, at least he could answer that without explicitly lying.

"She is not my girlfriend," he ground out, reaching over to take her hand in his. It wasn't for comfort or to insist on the point to her, he told himself. It was just a matter of falling into the roles that the two of them were to play, that was all. Nothing more. Really.

Her face lit up at that. He was torn between surprise at how cute she looked, agitation at his own desire to stretch the moment out for as long as possible, and an overprotective irritation at how quick she was to trust.

"So, how exactly do we do this?" she asked.

"Do this?" His words came out slowly, his thoughts still lingering on the conflict within himself.

"Yeah, are we supposed to snuggle up, or kiss, or am I supposed to get under the table and..."

That snapped him back to the present. His mouth suddenly felt inexplicably dry. "And?"

He'd thought that her teasing him with naughty words was the most erotic thing she could have done. He realized his error as soon as she blushed and looked away. The poor thing couldn't even make eye contact with him after saying something so bald and bold.

It would have been entirely in character for Harrison to tease her. Still, he felt a stab of pity that bordered on overprotectiveness. Heavens, what was the matter with him.

"No, nothing like that," he said, but his hand slipped across the table to settle atop hers. After all, he did have an objective here.

"Oh, thank goodness," she breathed out heavily, looking up to meet his gaze once more.

He wasn't sure if she was looking at him like he was the funniest man in the world or most charming or most charitable, but none of them were acceptable. At least, they weren't acceptable in any circumstances but the ones they currently found themselves in. Truly, she was playing the part magnificently and without even realizing it. Hopefully, he hadn't misjudged Natasha's capacity for murder like he'd misjudged her level of interest in him.

"For a second there, I was really worried, and I don't really do stuff like... that," she trailed off pitifully. Interesting. She couldn't even mention that sort of thing when she wasn't being ostensibly pressured.

What an uncomfortable sensation. Until a few minutes ago, Harrison had been quite secure in the notion that he liked his women experienced, jaded, and utterly shameless. It would seem that his body was rather at odds with his brain on this particular issue.

"Do you mean to say you've never done stuff like... that." He couldn't help but tease her, even going so far as to imitate her embarrassed fidgeting.

She sputtered, which may have been what he expected, but he most definitely didn't expect his own visceral pleasure at the sight.

"Come now, a pretty girl like you must have had a boyfriend or two."

How odd that he found his hand under the table making a fist. Being jealous of the hypothetical boyfriend of a woman that he'd only just met? That was beyond the pale, even for a possessive bastard like him.

Christ, he really needed to put a stop to this before she actually responded to his teasing.

"So, where exactly is Natasha now?" he asked conversationally. Still, he couldn't resist reaching over and taking her hand atop the table, trying very, very hard not to think about how soft her skin felt against his calluses.

She peered past him, seemingly far more engrossed in the answer to that question than the facts of what he'd just done. Anyone who wasn't holding her hand wouldn't have noticed how warm and trembling she was.

"Standing by the door and looking impatient. She's checking her phone and—"

"Got it."

Well, that wasn't a good sign. Harrison may not have spent all that long around Natasha, but he had picked up that she fidgeted with her phone when she was exceptionally frustrated. That really only made sense, considering the majority of his interactions with her had involved various levels of rage and indignation on her part.

Only then did he realize that an oddly heavy silence had stretched out between him and his odd partner of circumstance. One good questioning stare solved that quickly enough.

"Is... is her name really Natasha?"

Harrison blinked. "Of course. Why would I make something like that up?"

She waved her free hand frantically but still suitably subtly that it didn't attract too much attention. However, he was far more focused on the feel of her other hand.

"I wasn't accusing you of making anything up," she whispered hastily but then regained control of herself. "What I meant was that she doesn't really act like a Natasha."

That caught him off guard, and Harrison couldn't help but laugh. Just a moment too late, he realized his mistake. There was absolutely no way that his jilted ex could miss identifying him now. It wasn't like he laughed often, but he was invariably told that it was a surprisingly distinctive laugh. Judging by the peculiar expression on the redhead across from him, she concurred.

Once she regained control of her thoughts with a shake of her head, she continued. "I mean that I would have expected her to look cold instead of so fiery and impatient." She glanced past him but then did a double-take and stiffened.

"Oh my, she's headed right for us."

Chapter 3

How had Mia James gotten sucked into such a mess? One minute, she'd been leisurely sitting on the edge of exhaustion and exhilaration, watching the night owls of Vegas and easing into her vacation, and the next, the most striking man she'd ever seen had imperiously taken the seat across from her and pulled her into some sort of bizarre performance.

It was a performance, she was pretty sure of that now. There was no other explanation for why a simple girl like her would be involved in what could only be described as a passion play, especially one between two such astonishingly attractive people.

The more she thought about it, the more she decided that Natasha was actually a reasonably fitting name. Though the tall woman storming towards them was overflowing with righteous indignation, she was also downright majestic in form. High cheekbones, a thick fur coat that covered as much as the dress peeking out below didn't, and lengthy fingernails that nearly drew blood as they clenched against her skin, this was a woman that looked ready to commit murder.

And not for a moment did she doubt that the man across from her was the object of this woman's passion.

It was odd, he definitely wasn't anything remotely in the neighborhood of what she considered her type. He wasn't safe or charismatically funny in the disarming way that she preferred, but he caught the eye and demanded attention in a way that she'd never known before. Between his shaved hair and an endless supply of tattoos, he reeked of danger and risk-taking. Taken alone, every one of his features were among the last she looked for in a man, but taken together...

Mia swallowed and remembered that he was still holding her hand. Or rather, he forced her to remember by gently stroking his thumb against the softness that was her palm. Never before had she been quite so aware of the difference between two different textures and what they meant. She was soft and pampered, he was hardened and unafraid to get his hands dirty.

Of course, she couldn't help but wonder what kind of woman that such a man would choose. It was probably someone like his partner in this charade, the woman that was stalking towards them with fury in her eyes. Honestly, she was more than a little impressed, in spite of herself. This performance really was incredibly believable.

"Am I supposed to do anything?" she whispered under her breath just before "Natasha" reached the table.

But there was no time for him to reply. Natasha descended upon them, grinding her teeth nearly loud enough for Mia to hear. If nothing else, it did make her cheekbones stand out even more magnificently. If this little play had suddenly shifted to reveal that she was a member of ancient Russian nobility, Mia would have believed it in an instant.

"Harrison, fancy meeting you here." Her voice was low and dangerous, betraying not a hint of acting.

So his name was Harrison then. Then again, it probably wasn't his real name.

"Natasha? My my, what are the odds?" If she didn't know any better, Mia would think that he was genuinely surprised. However, after a couple minutes in the man's presence, she found herself able to recognize the dreadfully dry undertone to his words.

Unfortunately, that's when Natasha shifted her attention away from her acting partner. It wasn't so much that Mia was uncomfortable under her gaze, but more so that she grew painfully aware that his hand was still atop hers and showed no sign of moving.

And then, from somewhere deep inside her that Mia hadn't even known existed, she felt a surge of forwardness. She had come to Vegas to have a good time, and by golly, she wasn't going to back down from a challenge.

"Harrison, sweetie, who's this?" Mia asked in a sickeningly sweet tone, raising her second hand to layer atop his, making a Harrison hand sandwich.

She already had Natasha's attention, but now Harrison looked at her as if seeing her for the first time. The way his forehead wrinkled in confusion was just so adorable that she had to fight off the urge to giggle, but that would simply be unladylike. More to the point, it would ruin the show that these two were clearly putting on for her benefit. The least she could do was play along to the best of her meager abilities.

Oh wow, Natasha was really committed to her part. Half of her froze, and the other half shook with barely-contained rage. Her eyes burned with an urge to commit violence so fiercely that Mia very nearly recoiled. However, she was made of sterner stuff than that and even found herself enjoying this playing of a role that very much was not her own.

"I see how it is. You've already gone and found yourself a new plaything." Natasha's voice was low and quiet but venomous, nearly to the point of comedy. It was truly some of the best acting Mia had ever heard. Did this woman have a show? If so, she simply had to attend it before her vacation was over.

"Natasha, come now," Harrison cut in, his tone perfectly calming and conciliatory, as though he'd done this a hundred times before. Logically, he must have. "You knew that what we shared was just a bit of fleeting fun. It was a wonderful week, but you were going home, and I was staying here. I'm sorry if I led you to believe that my attention meant something deeper, but it really was just a fling."

Mia ached at those words, and she wasn't even the target! Oh, he was much too good at this, woe to any woman that found herself genuinely on the other end of his teasing temptation and rejection!

Natasha's hand shook as she raised it, and for a moment there, Mia thought that she might genuinely be about to find herself embroiled in a brawl. But then the imperious woman trembled, and the faintest hint of wetness shone in her eyes, then she turned about and stormed out.

All around, the few denizens of the cafe completely and utterly ignored this performance, which led Mia to believe that it was definitely an act. She'd wondered why she'd been lucky enough to be the audience participant, but now it all made sense. Everyone else here was a regular and had already seen it dozens of times over, or at least something like it, so they logically picked out the only tourist. It did not occur to Mia to wonder how she was immediately identifiable as a non-local and whether that might cause problems in the future.

From what Mia recalled about the layout of the hotel, the front entrance was several rooms and one large lobby away. That made it quite impressive when the sound of a loud slam reverberated loud enough to make her glass of water rattle.

"My, she's a very committed actress," Mia said quietly, even though there was no real reason to keep her voice down anymore.

Harrison looked at her oddly. Actually, now that she thought about it...

"So, what's your real name?" Mia pressed.

He frowned. "Beg your pardon?"

"You know— I mean...." Oh dear, was Harrison his real name? But... he looked nothing like a Harrison! And she'd been so sure.

But he didn't take offense, he just grinned. "It's really Harrison. Harrison Siegel, if you must know." He waited expectantly for a long moment as if she was supposed to recognize that.

"Er... it's a nice name?"

"Bugsy?" he pressed in turn. As to whether that was a name, a nickname, or some sort of car, Mia hadn't the faintest idea.

"Gesundheit?"

Once more, he surprised her by laughing instead of being annoyed. This time, it was a rich laugh, the same one that she'd heard earlier and longed to hear once more. It was downright perplexing that such a joyous sound could come from a man that looked like that, but there it was. And Mia still wanted to hear it once again. Perhaps she could figure out exactly what was amusing them, then use that to—

Harrison Siegel rose from the booth, surprising her with just how big he was. How had she not noticed when he'd arrived.

"Sorry, but I'm afraid I just realized I'm late for an appointment. I do apologize for the abruptness, and I hope that you enjoy the rest of your stay in Las Vegas."

And with that, he turned around and strolled nonchalantly right out of the cafe. If she hadn't been quite so enamored with watching him leave, Mia might have worked up the courage to call out after him and give him her number. Then again, she reflected as soon as he was gone and her senses had begun to work properly once more, it was all probably very intentional on his part. This was purely a performance, just a job on his part. He didn't want her name. To him, she was probably just one of a hundred, even a thousand girls that he had to charm and leave in his line of work.

But then again, it wasn't so bad to be alone with her thoughts once more. Mia had always enjoyed her time to process things, and the dim cafe was perfect for that. All around, men and women were slowly building up the willpower to confront the coming day or languidly relaxing after a rough night dancing up on stage. She imagined backstories for all of them, for the woman sitting on her lonesome to be a dancer near the end of her career, for the two men sitting together to be brothers reuniting for a weekend of fun after living on opposite sides of the country, for the older man and woman to be partners that had just rekindled the spark with a trip to the City of Sin.

Sighing contentedly, Mia ordered another decaf coffee and mulled over the planner in her phone. She only had a handful of days to make the most out of this trip before she returned to her dreary existence, so she'd have to be strategic in deciding how to spend her hours.

Big shows in the early evening? Obviously, and especially if it meant she might get to see Natasha and Harrison perform again.

A truly fascinating thought struck her: what if the pair were actually lovers? What if they were deeply dedicated to one another and did this for fun? How scandalous and also a little bit uncomfortable, which made Mia shy away from the thought. What was next on her list?

Did she really want a few afternoons of low-stakes gambling? It was tempting, but was it too tempting? Did she have the kind of addictive personality that might spiral into the high of winning and place bigger and bigger bets until she lost everything to her name and then some?

For a brief, salacious instant, she remembered a novel she'd read about a girl that fell so deeply into debt that there was only one way to repay the cold, hard man that held her life in his hands. Then again, calling it, a novel might have been overly generous. It had been a short and extremely satisfying read, though.

Mia sighed, this time for all the usual reasons. Fantasizing about being paid genuine attention from a man like Harrison was one thing, but she knew better than to hope for it to happen in reality. She knew a dangerous man when she saw one, and that was before she'd learned that he could lie as easily as he could speak. Call it acting if you want, but that was a man who knew how to toy with a woman's heart like a pro. She had no trouble at all believing that he was really capable of tossing a woman like Natasha aside.

But Mia James wasn't looking for a man. Rather the opposite, really. She'd come to Vegas hoping to forget, and so far, the city had done a damn fine job in that regard. Hopefully, the next few days would be even better, and the mere thought of that was enough to make Mia shudder in anticipation. Oh yes, this was shaping up to be the best week of her life, and it was only the first night.

Series by
J.F. Lowe

Masters of Highclere:
A Sailors Daughter
Coxswains Cuffs
Returning to Highclere
Medical Ménage

Masters of Highclere Forbidden Stories (Standalone)

Love Games:
Married Games
Revenge Games
Sinful Games
Connor (Love Games Trilogy - Novella)

Protecting Her Innocence (Standalone)

Jealous - Not Me! (Standalone)

Wickedly Innocent

Composing Sins
Recording Sins

Seduction In The City:
Seducing Austin
Seducing Philly
Seducing Vegas
Seducing Wall St
Seducing The Capitol
Seducing Chicago

Tis The Season For Romance - Anthology

Caught Under The Mistletoe - Anthology

Road to Love Series (Coming 2022)
Broken Love
Departed Love
Forbidden Love

More by J.F. Lowe

More by J.J. Lowe

Love Games

It's erotic, it's romantic, and wonderfully suspenseful.
Hold on tight and get ready for a wild ride!

Married Games

Matthew Davidson was everything she'd ever
dreamed of in a man and more. But two years after
marrying the construction mogul, Sarah's fairytale romance falls apart taking them to a place of sex, lies,
and murder. Sarah doesn't know whether she can trust
the man she married... or even herself.

Revenge Games

After finding out that in her husband past he liked
to share women with his best friend, Sarah realised
that she knew nothing about the man she married.
Now she is caught up in a game she didn't even know
she was playing.

Sinful Games

It's been five years and yet the scars still show on my body. My husband Matthew still wakes with night terrors each night and they have only gotten worse since our beautiful daughter Katherine was born. I want my husband back, our marriage back and I'm willing to do anything to get it. Even if it means submitting to Matthew's deepest desires.

This novel contains explicit sexual content, graphic language, and situations that some readers may find objectionable. Not intended for those under the age of 18.

A Sailors Daughter

A forbidden love. A secret desire. A deadly past. A fight for survival.

At seventeen she made her oath to Queen and country, but nothing could have prepared her for life as a navy recruit. As Jenna steps onto the parade ground for the very first time, her life changes forever when she meets the tall, dark and handsome Petty Officer Rhys Morgan.

Faced with her first night legally as an adult and her eighteenth birthday, Jenna has only seconds to choose between the loneliness of the navy base or to trust the Petty Officer. She had no idea what will be asked of her or the boundaries that will he would push as he introduces her to his secret life.

Petty Officer Rhys Morgan hasn't been so attracted to a woman like this in years. His life at sea as a Petty Officer meant his relationships never lasted, like his first marriage. But the little recruit intrigues him like no other. Failing to be able to keep his distance as her instructor, the little recruit soon becomes all that he wants, needs and craves.

This novel contains explicit sexual content, graphic language, and situations that some readers may find objectionable. Not intended for those under the age of 18.

About J.F. Lowe

I grew up in a country town in Central Queensland, Australia. As the fruit of a long line of military men and not much to do, it gave me plenty of time to create a fantasy world full of hot men and wild romances. It was only when I met my own hot alpha that I decided to share my love of books and writing with the world.

Nowadays, I in Brisbane, Australia and when I'm not writing, I can be found with a nice glass of wine and spends her time with her husband and holidaying with her three children. My favourite way to spend an evening is curled up on a couch next to my own hot alpha, reading and making the most of a quiet night in... well maybe not so quiet... if you read my books then you know what I mean.

Review

Thank you for reading my book, I hope you enjoyed it as much as I enjoyed writing it. Won't you please consider leaving a review? Even just a few words would help others decide if the book is right for them.

www.ingramcontent.com/pod-product-compliance
Lightning Source LLC
Chambersburg PA
CBHW070015120726
47909CB00003B/937